The House of Silence

by G. H. Teed

Illustrator: Eric Parker

First published in The Sexton Blake Library,
2nd series, Issue 253, Sep. 1930.

Stillwoods Edition

Stillwoods.Blogspot.Ca

Catalogue Information:
Title: The House of Silence
Author: G. H. Teed (1881-1938)
Illustrator: Eric Parker
First published in The Sexton Blake Library, 2nd series, Issue 253, Sep. 1930.
This Edition by: Stillwoods, 2021, (Doug Frizzle)
ISBN Canada: 978-1-989788-71-4
Blog: Stillwoods.Blogspot.Ca
Author Blog: http://ghteed.blogspot.com/
Storefront: http://www.lulu.com/spotlight/lulubook22
Copyright © Doug Frizzle and/or Stillwoods, 2021.
Cover adapted from the original.

Keywords: Sexton Blake, British fictional detective, Tinker

https://tinyurl.com/ve25d42s This link should go to a spreadsheet of all known Teed stories. The list is annotated with various information on the stories and my progress with recapturing the work. The library of Teed's stories increases almost daily. Check at the **Lulu.Com** for the latest arrivals. Search for Teed./drf

Cautionary Note: This series of books by Stillwoods are intended to make the stories of G. H. Teed, born in New Brunswick, Canada, available to collectors and researchers. The editor, or rather digitizer has not altered the original publication.

This story may contain language and racial terms that are not appropriate to today. I apologize for them; I know that the author was using his voice to excite and entertain an adventurous English audience. These works were published from 82 to 110 years ago. Most every work has characters of redeeming ethnicity within.

I hope you enjoy and share these stories; I have.

Doug Frizzle

It is noted that this is **ISBN request #201**. A hobby I certainly had never anticipated when I retired!

Other content: Not Guilty by Anon.; Crooks' Inventions (article)

A dramatic detective novel of thrills and sinister adventure, introducing Sexton Blake, the world-famous detective.

The HOUSE OF SILENCE

A dramatic
detective
novel of
thrills and sinister
adventure,
introducing
SEXTON BLAKE,
the world-famous
detective.

By G. H. TEED.

This is one of the first **Sexton Blake Library** issues I have done so here is a few words of the physical aspects of this issue made in 1930, well after the Great War and before WW2, —midway.

The issue is made of sheets 11" wide by 7" high, the sheet being folded, thus creating 4 actual pages. So a page with of 5.5" is created. Page numbering goes from 1-64 but with the cover pages there are actually 68 pages. One staple goes through the middle of the cover to the end page about 3/16ths inch from the spine. After 90 years the staples are usually absent but there is staining.

I believe this magazines are categorized as true 'pulps'; the quality of paper is not great, but also not so bad as some earlier years.

It is also notable that there is a cover image and a page 1 title image, that's all!

Comparison between magazines in 1930.

Below are the rough specifications for two of the Sexton Blake regular issues. It is notable that the size of the font is very small.

The House of Silence

By G. H. Teed

First published in The **Sexton Blake Library**, 2nd series, Issue 253, Sep. 1930.

Paper is 27.8cm or 10.94" double width (5.47"-single); height is 17.64cm or 6.94"

Pages are 68, with one staple through the face of the document. Octavo plus cover?

Font of the story is Century Schoolbook 7.

Words 43500.

Cost 10c from cover; 4 ½ d. from advertizing page.

The Twilight Feather Case

By G. H. Teed

Illustrated by

First published in the **Union Jack** magazine, Series 2, No. 1368, 4 January 1930.

Paper is 19.16cm or 7.54" wide (single page); 27.59cm or 10.86" height

Pages are 28, with two stapes through the spine.

Font is Century Schoolbook 7.5

Words 24900.

Cost 2d. from cover.

/drf

Chapter 1. The Gambler.

IN all his reckless, adventurous career Romer Walmsley had never been more completely broke than on the night when he staggered out of the dirty little South American river town of Honda.

He could not have told why he had stepped off at the place instead of continuing on down the broad river to the coast. There, at least, there was a chance of working his way to some other country, or at worst, of picking up some sort of temporary existence by beachcombing.

But ever since leaving the gold district of Medellin he had been sunk into a state of hopeless despondency that threatened to reduce him to such depths that he would never recover.

He told himself he must be getting old to allow himself to sink under the blows that previously would have been but a spur to urge him to fresh struggles. It was not that, for he was still on the sunny side of thirty-five. It was simply that ruin had overtaken him at the end of a long period, during which he had been living on his nerves and hope and on little else.

The few hundred dollars he had been able to save as a stake-out of some business that had come his way had been lost in trying to work a placer gold claim in the back district that had yielded just enough during ten months to keep him toiling on in hope of striking a rich pan. Then it had petered out in a night, so to say.

By the time Walmsley had paid off the few peons he employed and the trifling debts he owed he had little more than enough to get him down to the coast. He had no plans other than that. For twelve years or more he had been knocking about the world on the trail of adventure, trying to strike it rich through honest means. Men had told him at different times that if his principles could be smothered occasionally he would find his profits greater. But until this last smash Romer Walmsley had played a straight game.

Never before had he allowed himself to sink to the bitterness that now filled him. He had seen other men make a strike, clean up and then depart —men who would have jumped another prospector's claim as soon as one could say knife.

Fortune, he kept repeating as he came down river in the flat-bottomed steamer, fortune favoured the crooked. It wasn't worth while playing straight. What had he got, he asked himself? Where was he after all those years? He could show less than twenty dollars in money and the few rags on his back plus his Colts, a supply of ammunition and a few odds and ends that wouldn't fetch ten bolivars in Santa Marta.

He was in that dangerous mood of drifting into anything that met him, and with the weight of his disappointment, the finer temper of character that had carried him through so far, had become dulled.

It was the chance meeting with a well-to-do cattle-man on the steamer that was really responsible for his disembarking at Honda. This individual, a big, noisy, hard-drinking fellow who was travelling down to Cartagena on business and pleasure mixed, and who was anxious to begin the pleasure end of it as soon as possible —one whose time was his own as well, had persuaded Walmsley to come ashore and join him in a spree that was supposed to last the four hours during which the steamer would wait.

It had developed into a heavy bout of drinking and the steamer had departed on her way down river before Walmsley and his companion even saw the inside of the faro joint.

By that time Walmsley didn't care what happened. His companion was a free spender, and guessing in a way how it was with Walmsley, had insisted on footing most of the bill. He would have pressed a roll of notes on the Briton, but this Walmsley declined.

Thus they reeled into the faro joint where, in the heat of the game, they soon got separated. Walmsley was reckless enough by this time to break into his tiny capital and take a chance. Fortune was with him at the start, as it generally is before leading a gambler up the garden path to ruin.

His twenty dollars grew to a hundred, and this sum he added to again and again until he had fully five hundred dollars stowed away in his soiled white trousers.

Now, of course, was the time to stop. Had he needed any excuse he could have found it in the condition of his cattle friend, who was now speechlessly drunk and lying in a state of collapse on a rough form in one corner of the dingy native gambling den.

Walmsley told himself, indeed, that he would play only to the end of the "case" that was then being turned, and after that, win or lose, he would get his friend out into the air and straighten him up for the continuance of the journey down river. It didn't occur to him even now that a good deal of time had passed since they came ashore and

2

that the steamer was already many miles away.

He kept to his resolve, played to the last turn of the card from the "case," found he had reduced his winnings by only a few dollars and turning, looked for his friend. He had disappeared.

A few inquiries led him nowhere until a swarthy mestizo informed him that the "big senor" had departed some time since. Walmsley thinking he had gone to some place he knew to sleep off the bout, hesitated. A call from the faro table told him a fresh "case" was just about to be turned. He hesitated again and was lost.

Not even one winning turn did he make. From the moment of his second visit to the table the money drained steadily out of his pocket until he was reduced to less than the original small capital with which he had entered.

In one last desperate throw he tossed every remaining dollar on to the table, watching the turn of the "case" with cynical eyes. He had played the ten "to win." It was turned "to lose," and thus the remnants of his small stock was swept away.

Walmsley shrugged and turned away. He could have borrowed a further stake had he wished, but he knew he hadn't a hope of repaying should he lose. So dragging out the few small coins that had escaped the final raking he regarded them speculatively.

There was enough, with a small tip, for a bottle of native rum — unmatured, fiery stuff made on the local sugar plantations. He invested in a flask of this, and betaking himself to one end of the room drank it in three large measures.

On top of what he had already consumed that day it should have keeled him over. But it was probably the taut state of his nerves that kept him on his feet, for when he kicked open the half-swing doors and plunged into the cool —comparatively— night air he walked fairly steadily.

He hadn't a notion where to go for the night. Nor did he know how he would subsist in Honda until the next river boat came down two days hence. It was not the sort of place a white man should find himself on his uppers. But he was past worrying very much about that.

Taking out some rough tobacco leaves he rolled himself a cigar, and lighting it, made his way towards the riverside jetty. He was wondering what had become of the cattle-man, but he was never to set eyes an him again. Fate was on the point of making another turn of the wheel in Romer Walmsley's affairs.

While he had been in the faro joint, Walmsley was quite unaware that he had been under close and speculative supervision by a pair of unseen eyes. He knew nothing of the wine-shop in the opposite street that backed up against the rear of the faro joint, the two being owned by the same man and having more than one means of communication between them. Nor did he know of the big, flabby man who sat in a private room of the wine-shop studying an old bit of parchment beneath the smoky light of a hanging lantern.

No more did he know that the pair of eyes that had been watching him while he played, that had gauged shrewdly his losses and had seen his last indifferent attack on the flask of rum, belonged to a girl, whose alive skin proclaimed the southern blood in her veins even if her black eyes were not sufficient —a girl on whose shoulder was perched all during the period of her surveillance a gigantic macaw, whose age would have been found to be well over a hundred years had one been able to trace the course of its wicked life.

But Walmsley was in ignorance of the underplay of life about him. He did not know that, no sooner did he bang his way out of the joint, than the girl sped along a passage to the private room where the big man, a European, sat bent over his bit of parchment. His ears did not hear the whispers that passed between them; he knew not whence came the girl who approached him soon after as he lounged at the end of the jetty smoking, her head and shoulders concealed by a black mantilla.

He merely noticed absently that a woman was standing in the shadow, and thinking he knew her purpose, he turned away, intending to make off if she approached him. But a few moments later when she did speak there was some quality in her voice that held him where he was and brought his closer attention upon her.

"The senor is lonely?"

Walmsley made no reply.

The woman laughed softly.

"The senor regrets his losses at the game. But I do not come to offer my company out of sympathy. It may be that I have something else to offer which will interest the senor."

He gazed at her with new interest. So closely was the mantilla draped about her that he could not see even the dim outline of her features. Yet he knew by the voice that she was young. If she didn't

4

come to offer the sympathy of her companionship, then what did she want of him?

Before he could make any reply something swooped out of the gloom and whirled about his head. Thinking it was a giant vampire bat he threw up his arm to strike. But his hand found only empty air, and, as a squawking pandemonium broke out above him, he saw a phantom shape dip towards the girl and settle on her shoulder. Again that low laugh.

"It is nothing to fear, senor. It is only my pet macaw."

Walmsley cursed under his breath. The strain he had been under and the huge quantities of alcohol he had taken into his system were getting him nervy.

He would have moved away, but the girl put out a detaining hand.

"Wait, senor. I have no desire to pry into the senor's private affairs, but if it is a fact that the senor has lost all his money at the gaming table I can offer him something that will replace it many times over."

Walmsley pricked up his ears. He couldn't imagine what a Spanish woman of a place like Honda could offer him that would show financial profit, unless it were to cut the throat of some unwelcome admirer.

"I am afraid I am not eligible, senorita," he said gruffly, and again would have moved, away. But once more she detained him.

"Would the senor not be interested in treasure —Spanish treasure of many centuries? A man of courage and experience is needed, senor. If the senor can fulfil those conditions there is one waiting who would speak with him."

He pressed her for further details, but she would say no more than that he should learn all if he would follow her. As it didn't matter two straws now to Romer Walmsley what happened he shrugged and yielded.

He noticed that she led him past the faro joint where he had lost his money and down a narrow, dark passage that brought him round into a dirty, sandy lane that could only be called a street out of courtesy. More they dodged into a building which he saw readily enough backed against the rear of the faro joint. But he did not know until later that there was any connection between the two.

He noticed, however, that it was a wine shop into which he and his cattle friend had penetrated —among many others —during the day. He did not know that he had been under surveillance ever since, for he was quite unaware that a peon, who had travelled down as a deck passenger from he gold country, had pointed him out as a "gringo" who had lost his money mining.

But the girl did not pause in the wine shop. She led him along a dark corridor to the private room where the big man sat studying his bit of old parchment. And thus did Romer Walmsley first meet Junius Markheim, master criminal, who was to offer him wealth with one hand and snatch his freedom with the other. Had he been wise he would have fled then and there from the one who was to be his evil genius.

Chapter 2. The Fight.

IT is no part of this record to detail the temptation which caused Romer Walmsley to sink the scruples that would normally have kept him out of the scheme that Junius Markheim laid before him.

Markheim had a persuasive way that had inveigled many a man —and woman —before Walmsley came into his net. In most of the out-of-the-way places of the globe Junius Markheim had been seen at some time or other during the past twenty years, and each time he had added, either little or much, to the stake he was building up for a final retirement.

Like most people Walmsley failed to place his nationality. He revealed the polish of London and Paris when he chose, used a dozen different languages with equal fluency, could descend to the peon argot of the country he was now in as easily as any mestizo, and yet, all the time, radiated tremendous force.

He was huge physically, gross of mould, predatory of nose and possessed a pair of dark eyes as coldly dominating as anything Walmsley had ever seen.

Just what relation the girl stood in Walmsley couldn't guess at that first meeting. But with her shawl removed he saw that she was beautiful in a devilish, exotic way that could lure a man to ruin while she laughed at his antics. Yet she flinched under Markheim's stare, gave him a swift submission that told its own tale.

Later on Walmsley found that there were others who danced to the crack of Markheim's whip —mestizos, peons and what-not. But just now, on his first night in Honda, he and Markheim and the girl — whose name he found to be Carlotta —were alone; that is, except for the huge tangle of colour that was the macaw, a vicious beast between which it and Walmsley there flamed an instinctive hatred.

Three days after that interview with Junius Markheim, Romer Walmsley found himself one of a party of a dozen or more sailing down the great river in a powerful whale-boat bound for the island of San Miguel that lay a few miles off the coast.

Treasure was their objective —treasure of Spanish doubloons and pieces of eight, cathedral plate and precious stones— emeralds, the chief prize —emeralds that had been torn from the great deposits far back in the interior by the Indians driven on by the Spanish conquistadores.

Those emeralds, so Markheim informed him, lay in such quantity as to control the markets of Europe if one could gain possession. And only one thing stood between them and that achievement —the solitary, aged Spanish grandee who was the rightful owner, and who, like all his family for generations past, refused to dip into the riches to any greater extent than would provide the needs of a very modest way of life.

Don Edouardo de Santos was the seigneur of the island, where he lived with his only daughter and a few peons. The old piece of parchment that had come into Markheim's hands revealed the secret. It would be too easy to carry out the raid, he assured Walmsley, but he needed another European on whom he could depend. Walmsley was that man; he would receive a full half share for the part he played.

And Walmsley, thinking nothing of the almost defenceless old man and his daughter —desiring now only to feel the cool stones slipping through his fingers, put all the past behind him and went.

What followed remained with him for years as some fevered dream. There was the early morning landing in a little cove of the island. Then the vision of Don Edouardo, tall and thin and very aristocratic, appearing on the arm of a white-clad slip of a girl to give courteous welcome to the strangers.

There was Markheim's brutal demand that the treasure be handed over at once. Walmsley would never forget the cool dignity with which the old don had countered the demand, and then —everything seemed to break loose at once.

He could hear the crack of a pistol, thin on the morning air, could see the sudden collapse of Don Edouardo, could hear the anguished cry of the girl as she dropped to her knees beside him, and then the rush as feet kicked up the sand.

He had not anticipated cold-blooded murder. Yet he knew he was branded with the crime, although it was not his hand that had sent the old man to his death.

His protests to Markheim had been cut off with a sneer. Into the very midst of the hurly-burly of looking for the treasure came Carlotta's surreptitious offerings of her love. That was a thing to nauseate him. At any other time he would have used gentleness. Now he repulsed her with a snarl and forged for himself as terrible a spike of vengeance as ever was thrust into a man.

He did not see the De Santos girl again. He knew that Carlotta had led her from the scene. He was dull of mind as he went with the others to the spot where they expected to find the treasure. But the old parchment had lied. The cache was empty.

Then followed a tearing and rending of every likely spot on the island until Markheim emerged victorious. And when the great chest of treasure was torn open, to his profane gaze it proved even richer than he had hoped.

But one of the peons, faithful to the old don, had managed to get away from the island in a dugout. Making the mainland safely, he had stirred up friends of his master's, who had acted swiftly.

It was not until long after that Romer Walmsley knew how Junius Markheim had evaded that attack, and managed to get clear with the treasure. But he learned months later that it was Carlotta's vengeance that painted him as the villain of the piece.

So unexpected, so swift the treachery that he was seized before he had a chance to defend himself. He had no opportunity to make a statement. He was dragged away and thrown into a foul prison in Cartagena charged with the whole crime.

Vague news reached him that Markheim and Carlotta with the De Santos girl had disappeared. He puzzled why the girl should have joined with her father's murderers, but the truth of that did not become revealed for a long time after.

Several years passed during which he sweated in the foul hole, kept alive by one thought and one thought only —the determination to escape and find Junius Markheim.

It was a revolution that gave him his chance. When the rebels broke into the prison and released those who were confined Walmsley was among the liberated. Gladly enough he joined in the fighting, and it was the loot that came his way as the result that gave him the necessary stake to carry out his intention.

It was not until nearly another year had passed, however, that he found an opportunity to leave the country and make his way to Europe. There, he had made up his mind, he would begin his search, for he remembered that Markheim had said more than once that when he had enough he would retire to the hub of civilisation where he had taken care to commit no misdeeds that would bar him from residence.

And thus, on a day in early summer, Romer Walmsley came to the house of Sexton Blake, the famous detective of Baker Street, London.

Blake was at work in the consulting-room with his assistant, Tinker, when a tall, bearded man in tweeds was shown in. The card that had been brought to Blake by Mrs. Bardell, the housekeeper, was, the detective noticed easily enough, newly printed, not even engraved. That, plus the bronzed appearance of his visitor and the general manner so distinct from one accustomed to civilisation, made it easy enough for Blake to guess that he had landed but recently in England.

He studied his man quietly while he got settled, and, taking out a pipe, filled it from Blake's small keg of tobacco. Then:

"I've heard a good deal about you, Mr. Blake," he said in low, pleasant tones, "so I've come to you, knowing hardly a soul in the whole of England. I want to find a man."

"That sounds easy or —the reverse," responded Blake, with a smile. "Suppose you let me have some particulars, Mr. Walmsley."

"I will; and I'll be as brief as I can."

Then he began, and gave a short sketch of his wandering, adventurous life up to the time when he had struck complete failure in the gold district of Medellin in South America.

"Ever play faro, Mr. Blake?" he asked suddenly.

"A good many times," admitted the detective.

"Well, then you'll understand. I was coming down the river, making for the coast, when I got off at Honda. That was my undoing."

"I know Honda slightly. Was it at the old shack near the jetty that you played faro?"

"It was; then you know it?"

"I do."

"Well, that was where I hit bottom."

He then related how he had played, had won, had returned to the faro table and had lost every sou except a few loose coins which he had thrown away on a bottle of country rum.

Followed the story of his meeting with the girl Carlotta, of his introduction to Junius Markheim, and of the plot to raid the island of San Miguel and carry off the De Santos emeralds.

Then his betrayal, the flight of Markheim and Carlotta with the De Santos girl, his own incarceration in prison, his escape during the revolution, his getting together of a stake through looting, and finally his departure for England in search of Markheim.

"I don't know whether he is in England or not," he said when he had reached that point. "I have a hunch that he has settled down either in this country or in France. But I want to find him, and I fancy you can put your hands on him quicker than I can. You have an organisation that would cover such business, haven't you? I've got a bit of money sown away, Mr. Blake, and I'll pay your fee."

Blake's face had been impassive during the latter part of the recital. And now his voice was quite non-committal as he said:

"It is true that I have built up such an organisation, Mr. Walmsley, but before I place it at your disposal I must know a little more about things. Just why do you wish to find this man Markheim? I know that you desire to gain possession of some of the treasure with which he absconded, but —what else?"

"I'll kill him with my own hands if he baulks me," muttered the other. "I've waited a long time to find him."

"Well, you needn't go any farther. You can take it that I flatly refuse to lend myself or my organisation to any such purpose. You seem to be under a misapprehension, Mr. Walmsley. My business is to prevent crime, not to encourage it. If this man Markheim has been guilty of criminal practices, then there is a law, and I have no doubt the Government of the South American republic in question would lend you every aid in tracking him down. Whether they would give you a share of any treasure that might be recovered is another matter. But you do not seem to have paused to reflect that the treasure belongs to neither you nor Markheim. It seems to me to be the property of the girl— the daughter of the old man who was shot down. Murder is an ugly thing, Mr. Walmsley, and I will have nothing to do with those who have any hand in it, no matter how innocent they may be in deed."

"But the girl is with him," protested his visitor.

"That may be. But you do not know if she accompanied him willingly. It may be that she was forced in some way to join him and his party. If he and the woman of whom you have spoken were clever enough to have you thrown into prison they would be quite capable of inducing the girl to accept some story. —No, Mr. Walmsley, you have come to the wrong place. Go to the London legation of the country in question, or ask advice at Scotland Yard. Without offence, your own position in the affair up to the time of the shooting of the old man does not appear to do you too much credit. I am sorry, but there it is. I do not think we need prolong the discussion."

Romer Walmsley left the house in Baker Street a very snubbed and puzzled man. Living so long in the wild places his sense of right and wrong had become dulled; his conception of the ethics of crime had got twisted grotesquely.

So imbued had he been with the idea of vengeance, so wronged did he feel at the manner in which Markheim had swindled him, and so hardened had he become to shooting and violent death that he had entirely lost sight of his own responsibility in the affair of Don Edouardo's murder.

Sexton Blake had given him something to think about, and, had Fate left him to stew in his own juice for a few days, there was a chance that he would get an entirely different perspective of his wrongs.

But at this point Fate stepped in once more, joggled his elbow just as he walked into Oxford Street, and, happening to glance up, he saw in a luxurious limousine the very man he was seeking —Junius Markheim.

And by ten o'clock that same night Romer Walmsley, through the simple process of trailing Markheim in another car, had learned where he was living.

That discovery was enough to banish from his mind all that Sexton Blake had said. His desire for vengeance returned with greater force than ever. Yet he did not make the mistake of plunging into some precipitate move.

Carefully he laid his plans, for he knew that Markheim would not fly easily from the place to which he had become anchored. Two more days passed before he was ready, but then, garbed in the same rough tweeds, and carrying a knapsack on his back as if starting on a walking tour, he set out from London on a motor-cycle to the meeting he had planned for so long.

Had he dreamed of what was to be the outcome of that journey he might have paused and given heed to what Sexton Blake had said.

THE man in tweeds caught his first glimpse of the house as he breasted the hill.

The whole of the little valley lay patterned before him with the big pile of mellowed Sussex brick, the only habitation in sight, calmly arrogant with the serene dignity of great age.

The traveller shifted his haversack to a more comfortable position and leant on a long staff.

"So this is the pleasant retreat where you have hidden yourself all these years, Junius Markheim," he apostrophised the distant house. "An estate worth having, Junius —worth having."

He removed the briar that had been clenched between teeth that showed white against the grizzled blonde of beard and moustache, knocked out the ashes against his staff, and thrust the pipe into the left side-pocket of his coat. The act seemed to remind him of something, for, allowing the staff to lie against his shoulder, he felt in the right side-pocket until his fingers curled round the butt of a flat automatic pistol.

He drew out the weapon covertly, giving a sharp glance at the safety catch, before returning it. Then, with his eyes fixed on the dappled patches between him and his objective, where the early afternoon sun painted the shadows of the great oaks and elms, he started on again, humming an odd little three-note tune as he went.

Midway along the valley he came to an old stone bridge that spanned a tiny stream. From the other side of this the road led to a pair of big wrought-iron gates which were secured with a heavy padlock. On the left was a small thatched lodge and a small wicket. The windows on that side of the lodge were open to the summer day, but though the traveller pulled at what he took to be a bell-rope, and shouted, his summons went unheeded.

Impatiently he lifted the latch of the small gate and passed through. No one challenged him, so he continued up the broad sweep of the driveway until the house, which had been hidden by the trees, once more came into view.

The parkland through which he walked was close-cropped, as if sheep or cattle had been pastured there recently. Closer to the mansion the terraces and gardens betrayed every sign of attentive hands. The edges of the paths were cut cleanly fresh; the grass borders were shaved to a perfect level. Yet no sign of a gardener did he see.

The windows in their leafy vine settings were open, with the curtains moving lazily in the slight breeze that reached them. Smoke ascended in two plumes from chimneys in the rear quarters, marking kitchen industry of some sort.

The traveller passed the end of one line of terraces and continued on to the main porch, his approach being perfectly open and assured. Yet now he carried his long staff in his left hand, his other being in that side-pocket of his coat where the automatic lay.

Two short flights of stone steps led to the wide, deep porch, the open door of which revealed a large, panelled hall. The man in tweeds frowned under the peak of his cap at the silent invitation. Half-way down the hall an ancient staircase of black oak rose to the floor above. On either side were closed doors; beyond the staircase, a huge open brick fireplace, summer cold, and other shadowy doors, closed.

On the left of the entrance was a brightly polished knob, and on the right a modern brass bell-push; on the centre panel of the open door an old-fashioned brass knocker, gleaming from recent rubbing.

The man in tweeds dragged at the knob, rousing a distant jangling, which died away fretfully. But the only sound that followed was the faint ticking of the big clock half-way down the hall.

He brought his left arm across his body and pressed the bell-push. Somewhere beyond one of the closed doors the gong shrilled in muffled violence. A second and a third time he pushed his thumb on the button, but, beyond waking the distant echoes, secured no response.

Desisting, he surveyed the dignified symmetry of the hall. He had travelled for many years and covered many thousands of miles to effect this moment. Time and again he had speculated on how his meeting with Junius Markheim would be set. He had visualised it in almost every conceivable form possible in savage wastes and civilised restraint. Yet never had he foreseen this. There was something odd about this spacious house, with its open door and windows, that gave him pause more than any visible threat.

Once more he tested bell-pull, button and knocker, the big brass head sounding in a terrific clatter as he banged it on the swinging door. But jangle and shrill gong and thunderous booming died away into the same drowsy silence, with only the steady ticking of the old clock to complain.

The visitor set his staff and haversack in a corner of the porch and took a cautious step over the threshold. Another and another he essayed, until he was midway between two doors on either side. Then, inhaling, he emitted a coo-ee that roused the stilled echoes of the old hall and rose ebbingly up the stairs to unseen regions. Still —silence.

Suddenly he spied a big brass gong and padded hammer just beyond the grandfather's clock. Striding towards it, he set up a hullabaloo that seemed it must waken a corpse if such there were in that house of silence. From drumming roll it lifted to a racket that would have shamed a tom-tom, then faded back to mellow trembling, to die suddenly as he laid the padded stick against the quivering diaphragm.

Warily the man watched the closed doors. They stood, mute barriers, revealing nothing. With a purposeful movement he made for the first one that was on his left in entering, and, without ceremony, turned the handle.

The pushing open of the door revealed to him a delightful apartment with flowery chintz-covered furniture. It was long, passing another closed door which he knew to be the second on the left as he had stood at the entrance. There was every sign of recent occupancy —a work-basket on three legs and some tumbled bits of material being the most evident signs and revealing the dilettante industry of a woman.

But of such person there was no sign.

The man, who still clutched the handle of the door, retreated and turned to the opposite side of the hall. He wasted no time now in any attempt at formality. Turning the handle of the first door, he sent it flying inwards, his gaze encountering the chaste blue and silver of a music-room. Here again there were hints of normal household routine, for a sheet of music was on the stand, an open portfolio lay on a bench, and a violin and bow stood against the bulging leg of the instrument. It was the latter that brought forth one word from the lips of the stranger.

"Junius!"

Backing out warily, he passed down the hall and pushed open the next door. This time the dim coolness of a dining-room, silver and walnut gloaming richly. But no hint of human presence.

He faced the closed doors at the end of the hall, selecting the one farthest on the left. His boots sounded loudly as he strode towards it, scarring slightly the polished hardwood. But no challenge gave him pause.

Once more he turned a handle and pushed abruptly. But this time it was as if he had unlocked the secret spring that governed the house; for, immediately, there came a sharp explosion, and something struck him with stunning force just over the heart.

He staggered against the jamb of the door, glimpsing the seated figure at the desk with a pistol pointing straight towards the spot where one must stand on entering. Trigger and target had been synchronised perfectly. It was as if the figure seated behind the desk had been waiting patiently for the inevitable appearance of the person who was roaming about the house, waiting to kill him quickly, ruthlessly, before a single word could pass.

But, strangely enough, though the stranger staggered, he did not go down. Instead, he dragged out his own weapon and, lurching into the room, began shooting as fast as finger could flex. No reply came from the figure at the desk. Into the midst of the bearded, spectacled countenance the man in tweeds sent his shots until the automatic was empty. It was appalling in its shattering suddenness. And not until the figure in the chair lurched to one side and slumped to the floor did he advance farther; he stood there with the empty weapon in his hand, watchfully waiting.

But the falling of the body released his tensed muscles. Moving forward, he passed round the desk and bent over the prostrate form, his eyes fixed in sombre satisfaction on the back of the sprawled figure.

"You thought you were ready for my coming, Junius," he said at last. "It was a clever trap, but just a little too wide open."

He bent lower to turn the figure over. At the first contact a startled expression came into his grey eyes; then he emitted a single, terrible curse, for, as the loose head flopped to one side, he discovered the "dead man" to be naught but a form of moulded wax.

And then a deep, evilly-amused chuckle brought him to his feet.

Chapter 4. *The Invisible Barrier.*

JUNIUS MARKHEIM stood at one end of the long room.

His bulk was as enormous as ever; his amazingly grotesque ugliness of features unchanged. In the light of the place his square, black beard seemed still unflocked with grey. He was smiling with his lips and mocking with his pale blue eyes.

The man in tweeds lifted his weapon again and remembered it was empty. He started towards Markheim, slowly, warily. Markheim's ease of posture made him suspicious of another trap.

His hands came up as if ready to attack or defend; his fingers clubbed the automatic. And then he crashed into an invisible barrier, solid, hard, transparent.

Junius Markheim chuckled again. The stranger reeled back, staring in angry bewilderment. Close to him now was Markheim, yet a solid wall stood between.

The man in tweeds lifted a fist and struck out. His knuckles crashed into the invisible barrier. He moved closer and passed a hand along the surface.

"Glass."

"Of course, Walmsley."

The voice sounded as Markheim's lips moved, but seemed to Walmsley to impinge upon his eardrums from above or from one side. Markheim walked forward leisurely and stretched out his hand. It seemed incredible to Walmsley that it would not, could not touch him. So cunningly had the lighting of the room been arranged, that even now he could not be sure of the glass wall between them unless he felt the smooth contact.

He watched while Markheim passed his hand up and down the surface.

"Rather neat, Walmsley, don't you think?" he jeered. "It doesn't conceal us from each other's sight, but prevents mischief, eh? My own invention, and no bullet can penetrate it. And that reminds me — you were hit as you came in the door; why didn't it put you out? Are you wearing a bullet-proof shirt? All right, don't answer if you feel that way. But now that you have come after these years, we had better get down to cases. What do you want? I shall hear you quite easily if you speak, because there is a microphone on each side of the glass."

Walmsley backed away and, in full view of Markheim, slipped a

17

fresh clip of cartridges into the automatic. He did not attempt to shoot yet. He was prepared to believe Markheim's statement that the glass barrier could not be penetrated by a bullet. Junius Markheim was not the sort to be careless about a point like that.

"You know why I've come," he said quietly. "I want the share you diddled out of me, and I want an extra slice for the time I spent behind the bars. I've been looking for you for years, Junius, and I'm ready this time for any trick you can pull. It's going to cost you a lot to pay that old debt, but you've taken good care of what you got away with, if this place is anything to go by. I've got you cold, Junius, and you're going to pay."

"Big words, Walmsley, big words! You're entirely at my mercy. I knew you'd come some day —or night, but whatever the hour I was ready. I've had you watched ever since you landed. But I'll show you something first. I know you'd like to see Carlotta."

He turned as he finished speaking and walked heavily to a door in the far corner of the room. Walmsley could hear the soft thud of his heels on the thick carpet despite the glass barrier, so clearly did the microphone magnify every minute sound.

Markheim opened the door and disappeared. Walmsley turned and surveyed the space behind him. His way of retreat seemed clear enough. But he wasn't going that way yet. He hadn't come all those miles through several years to be scared off by any bag of tricks Markheim could display. He knew well enough that he stood on the brink of death, but he had expected to face that fate which was far preferable to the stench of the Spanish-American prison into which Markheim and the traitorous Carlotta had betrayed him.

He turned back as a new sound reached him. The door on the other side of the glass barrier was opening and Markheim appeared once more. He stood aside ceremoniously while a woman of sultry, exotic beauty swept in. The years had dealt lightly with her, despite the proneness of her race to mature early and fade quickly.

She was dressed in the same flame coloured silk she had always favoured. It contrasted well with her raven black hair and dark eyes. And on her shoulder was the same evil bird that Walmsley remembered so well, a brilliantly-hued macaw whose evil little eyes fixed on him at once in recognition. There was a commotion of feathers as the bird left its perch and soared towards the glass barrier, shrieking and cursing at the man on the other side.

The woman called it back, scolding it affectionately as it obeyed and clung once more to her shoulder. But it still continued to revile Walmsley, its beady eyes full of stark hatred.

Markheim's ugly face was crinkled with intense amusement.

"You see, Walmsley, even Chico has been watching for you."

Walmsley paid no attention. He was looking at the woman whose eyes were half veiled by heavy lids. He was remembering the last time he had faced her. He could still see the smoky lantern that hung in the dingy wine shop and the stained bit of parchment that was to bring wealth to all of them, a rascally crew, himself as bad as any. He could feel again the warmth of Carlotta's breath as she leaned close to him, murmuring words of love. He had given her no attention; he had paid dearly for the slight.

They had broken him. Markheim, like the ugly spider he was, had watched the byplay, had twisted the woman's insulted pride to his own purposes. And now —

"Carlotta shall decide," he heard Markheim saying. "Look at him, my dear —our gaolbird. He makes demands. He comes with threats. What shall we do with him, Carlotta?"

She smiled slowly, stroking the macaw.

Then she spoke, in Spanish:

"It would be a pity to disappoint him. Give him hospitality, Junius. Show him what we brought from the island. Then send Chico to amuse him. Chico's beak is a scimitar that will tear his throat."

Markheim was standing near a table. Now he pushed his hand across it as if to choose a cigar from an open box that lay there. Still watching the woman, Walmsley did not see the hand press gently for a moment on a part of the polished surface before the fingers closed on one of the weeds. Nor did he hear any sound as a whole section of the floor behind him disappeared from view. Not even in the smooth surface of the glass barrier was there any reflection of the gaping expanse that lay between him and the door by which he had entered.

His attention was wholly on Carlotta. Markheim was a known quantity for all his bag of tricks. The woman was an enigma, always had been unfathomable. Walmsley couldn't have told at any time if her approaches had been dictated by passion or some subtle calculation. And now there was something in her gaze that chilled him to the first hint of fear he had known since entering that house.

He wanted suddenly to get away. No precipitate attack would

gain him his ends here. They were too well prepared. He had counted on Markheim, but had not anticipated that Carlotta would still be a factor of such importance.

He backed away from the barrier and lifted his pistol. At his movement the macaw rose once more on wing, and, screaming evil invectives, hurled itself against the barrier in demoniacal fury. Walmsley hoped the creature would beat out its life in its insensate rage to get at him. The bird seemed to have an uncanny knowledge of the rebuff suffered by its mistress; it seemed to Walmsley that the very spirit of darkness must animate it.

Carlotta called to it sharply. For once it disobeyed her. Junius Markheim stood smiling, watching. Walmsley, in a sudden burst of purpose to test the barrier and bring the bird down, raised his pistol and fired. The bullet crashed against the glass, leaving scarcely a mark. There was a tinkling sound as, in the ricochet, it splintered a vase on the desk.

Walmsley retreated another step. Carlotta had stopped calling to the macaw. Markheim was no longer smiling. Both seemed intent on watching Walmsley. A curious sense of apprehension filled him. They knew something that was hidden from him. There was a menace hanging over him that was imminently threatening. A shiver ran down his spine and sudden beads of sweat moistened his forehead.

Still those two on the other side of the glass barrier watched him with an intentness that became more and more acutely disturbing. For a moment panic threatened to possess him. Then, pulling himself back to control, he again raised the pistol and shot deliberately. Once more the bullet failed to penetrate the thick transparency, ricochetting in a way that was dangerous only to Walmsley.

He backed another step.

In a flash, Markheim made a leap towards the invisible barrier. It was a movement of such suddenness that Walmsley involuntarily went back another pace.

"Look out!"

It was Markheim who shouted the words. Walmsley had the desk in mind. He would feel safer at that end of the room with a wall behind him. The odd expression in Carlotta's eyes was even more baffling than before. The pair were about to spring some fresh devilry, but Walmsley could got no hint of what it might be or from what direction it might come.

He retreated another step, but this time his foot came down upon nothing. He lurched, plunged backwards, firing a shot desperately as he plunged through the opening in the floor. He heard the crash of the weapon echoed by Markheim's loud laugh, Carlotta's low ripple, and the excited screeching of the macaw.

Then he tobogganed into violent oblivion.

Chapter 5.   *The Girl in White.*

JUNIUS MARKHEIM mounted the stairs with a step that was pantherishly light for one of his bulk.

From the first floor he climbed to the second, and, passing down a long hall, knocked at a door. Without waiting for any response he turned the handle, and entered a long, low-ceilinged sitting-room furnished in extreme comfort.

In a chaise-longue lay a girl dressed in white, with a light, white woollen rug across her limbs. Despite her paleness and lassitude of manner, she was very beautiful, with soft hair that gleamed like spun gold where the afternoon sun came through a barred window. Her eyes, deep blue, with a haunting expression, turned towards the door as Markheim appeared. At the same moment a middle-aged woman, with harsh features that were not softened by the severe black dress she wore, opened another door, and stood on the threshold regarding the man.

Markheim smiled ingratiatingly at the girl.

"Well, and how are we to-day, senorita?"

The girl lowered her lids wearily.

"About the same, I think. But something has happened. Sometimes I feel as if I were going to remember things. There is an influence which I feel."

Markheim regarded her keenly. Now that he studied her more closely he could detect a difference in her manner. There was a restlessness that was new; he could see a slight patch of colour in her cheeks. He glanced sharply, inquiringly, at the woman in black. She revealed no more response of expression than a stone.

Markheim drew up a chair and sat down, taking the girl's hand.

"I am glad to hear you speak in this way, Julia. I have always told you that time would do wonders. But do not try to force things. Let them adjust themselves naturally. You shall go for a drive later."

She glanced towards the barred windows, and shivered slightly, though the room was uncomfortably warm.

"If you wish, senor. But I am troubled. There have been moments when it seemed that everything was coming back. My father —"

"Don't speak of that now, Julia. You have been ill, and must not let things worry you. It will all be right soon, and it won't be long now before I take you back to the island."

She sighed, a look of longing coming into her eyes.

"The island —you promise? I know things would all come right again if I could go back."

"You shall. I promise you that as soon as I finish my business here we will go. But you must remember that I told you there are your own affairs to be settled as well."

He gave a sidelong glance towards the grim figure in black. The woman had drawn nearer now, and was standing just behind the girl's chair. Not for a single moment did she take her gaze from Markheim's face. He bent over the girl again and stroked her hand. She flinched a little under the touch, and had Junius Markheim looked at the grim-faced woman then he would have seen something violent flame in her eyes. But he missed it; he was too intent on furthering his purpose with the girl.

The girl shook her head slightly.

"Not yet," she murmured. "I will do what you wish when I am better. Why must I be worried about these things?"

Something caused him to frown, but only for a moment, his voice was softly insinuating as ever when he answered her.

"It is only a formality, as I have told you. There is nothing to worry about. It is only your signature two or three times, a few moments at most. Come, Julia, agree to do this to-day, and I will take you back to the island very soon —within a month."

"I will see. If I could understand what it is I feel to-day! Something has happened, I know."

Again his glance went to the woman behind the chair, but he learned nothing there. He rose, patting the girl's hand.

"I will take you for a drive, and after, perhaps, you will sign the papers."

"Perhaps."

He signalled surreptitiously to the woman as he turned towards the door. She followed him and passed through into the hall. Once the door closed all his suavity of manner dropped from him. His face was twisted, and his eyes blazing with anger as he grasped her wrist roughly.

"By Heaven, I believe you are up to some hanky-panky! If you are double-crossing me I'll throttle you, do you hear?"

Her arm was twisted back, but she betrayed no emotion of pain. She stood, unresisting, her eyes fixed on his.

"Speak, confound you!" he snarled in a whisper. "She could do the job quite all right if she wants to. What have you been saying to her?"

"Nothing!"

It was the first time the woman's lips had moved since Markheim's appearance. He flung her away from him. She staggered against the wall, but seemed to regard the brutality as nothing. Thus they stood for the space of a full half-minute, her eyes unfaltering under the threat of his.

"You heard what I said, you black death's head! I've stood for you and your demands just too long. If you try to queer my game now I'll kill you —get that straight! I'll wring your neck like I'd wring a chicken's."

"Who came to-day?"

"What's that to you?"

"Maybe nothing; but she has been restless. She has felt something. Who came?"

By the sheer monotony of her voice she seemed to force him to answer.

"Walmsley!" he snapped curtly.

She nodded her head slowly.

"I thought so. I knew he would find you. What has happened?"

"He's where he is going to stay. Don't you worry about Walmsley. I was ready for him, and Carlotta is able to look after him when I am not here."

"She was ready to look after him in a different way not so long ago," she responded.

He threw up a hand as if he would strike her. She did not flinch, just stared at him in the same dead way. He swung round with an oath.

"You get her fixed to sign those papers," he ordered, in a low tone. "If she doesn't toe the mark by to-night I'll find means of making her do so. If I can't, Carlotta can, and then you'll be at a loose end. Remember what I said. If you are trying to double-cross me Heaven help you!"

He strode down the hall, while she watched him go. When he had disappeared from view she lifted the wrist he had clutched and gazed at it for a few moments. Then her hand went inside her dress and she drew out a long, thin stiletto. She ran a finger along the smooth,

24

polished steel.

"You were very near to it to-day," she whispered, "very, very near. But not yet —not yet. It's got to be both of you."

She thrust the stiletto back under her dress and re-entered the room. The girl watched her with an animation in her glance that had been entirely absent while Markheim was present.

"Is he gone?'

"Yes."

"Have I got to drive to-day?"

"He says so."

"But he will make me sign. I could tell he is getting impatient."

"You do as I say. I've told you before I haven't any love for you, and I don't care whether you sign away everything you possess. But if you do you're a fool. He and the other will get it. It can't be long now, because something has happened. Keep up your refusal."

"Something has happened. I knew it. I could feel it. What is it?"

"Something that I've been waiting for for three years. We'll be out of this soon, or we'll be murdered."

And with that the grim-faced woman moved to the window and stood listening with strained attention.

WALMSLEY struck hard bottom with stunning force.

Had the drop been deeper he would have smashed half the bones in his body. As it was, he lay where he had pitched on his shoulder, with every atom of breath knocked out of him, his diaphragm heaving up in sharp agony, his senses swimming.

He was blind or in utter darkness. What light might have come down through the open section of the floor above through which he had descended so precipitately had been abruptly shut off by the closing of the trap.

With the first lessening of the inward agony he essayed to get his body straightened out, and acquire some idea, through touch, as to the nature of his immediate surroundings. His fingers encountered smooth wood, softish planed stuff that felt like pitch pine. It might be a cellar roughly lined with such material; it might be a hidden room constructed for some other purpose as well as serving as a receiving place for any victim of the trap.

His hands reached out farther, only to be seized in a vice-like grip. Until that moment Walmsley had no idea that he was not alone in the hole. He dragged back, the distasteful contact with unknown flesh lending him sudden strength. But a heavy body followed the clutching hands, and before he could do aught save struggle futilely, he was turned over and held while other hands trussed him, arms and legs, with swift efficiency. Then he was thrown violently down, to learn what he might from the vague sounds that followed for a few moments ending with what suggested itself to Walmsley as the closing of a door.

If he expected Junius Markheim to visit him and sit in triumphant judgment he was doomed to disappointment. Not another sound reached him. No footsteps were audible overhead; no vague murmur of household activities penetrated to the pit of blackness in which he lay.

He did not fool himself that Markheim was wasting any time wondering just what his fate had been. The unseen creatures who had been waiting for him to arrive via the floor drop would make their report. He had to admit that Junius was as thorough as ever. Yet it served no good purpose now to tell himself that he should have approached in a more circumspect manner. Junius had been ready for him for years. He knew he would come, and it wouldn't have mattered at what hour of the day or night he turned up.

Markheim had displayed the same efficiency in the old days. Going back in his mind Walmsley couldn't put his finger on a loose thread that Junius had left sticking out from the moment he had first met him in the hotel in South America until, with the old parchment plan in their possession, they had sailed in the whaleboat to the island where the De Santos treasure was reputed to be buried.

The vision of that morning rose vividly before him —the picture of old Don Edouardo do Santos, tall and lean and white-bearded, leaning on the shoulder of the young girl, his aristocratic face defiant and scornful; the shameful part he himself had played in the orgy of looting when Don Edouardo was shot dead while still clutching at his daughter; the girl's shriek of anguish, his own protest to Markheim, the treachery of the master-criminal and Carlotta when they reached the mainland again, and he was thrown to the wolves on the charge of killing Don Edouardo. The high lights had become blurred while he lay in the fetid prison, but now they returned, clear-cut as ever.

It had been a long trail and puzzling. What was Julia de Santos doing with Markheim and Carlotta? That she had travelled to England with them he had learned after his escape from prison. And with them had gone that great mahogany chest of jewels, the De Santos treasure collected in the days when the Spanish Main was the lure of Elizabethan adventurers.

No one disturbed his thoughts. In the pitch blackness it was difficult to make more than a rough guess at the passage of time. The acute discomfort of his bonds was getting more and more agonising; his extremities throbbed as if the locked-up blood would burst its walls. And there came the inevitable thirst, burning of the throat that seemed to crave more and more vehemently for one blessed draught.

It was impossible for him to fix his mind on anything but Junius Markheim. Round and round that physically gross entity they revolved. He knew now that Junius had planned for his coming, just as he had planned his undoing three years before. There didn't seem a single loose nut in the man's whole thinking apparatus; not a carelessly laid brick in the structure he had built up.

This cellar in which he lay; the trapdoor through which he had been dumped like a sack of corn; the dummy figure of wax at the desk with the weapon trained on the door and synchronised for discharge by electrical contact so that it must shoot straight and true at the person who entered. In that one thing could he say he had bested Markheim —in his knowledge of the man's capacity for treachery and his own forethought in wearing a bullet-proof shirt.

But Markheim had not counted on the first trap being infallible. There was the sliding partition of thick glass behind which he could stand triumphantly secure while Walmsley was again befooled; then the springing of the next trap that had acted with all the precision Junius had planned. And now, lying in the darkness of those invisible surroundings, Romer Walmsley was quite certain that had the second trap failed a third was ready to hand.

His mind came out of the confused circle of thought at the sound of faint scurryings. His first idea was that rats were running about and would soon be upon him. Then subtly he got the feeling that a human presence was close to him.

The intense blackness palpitated with slight but definite waves that struck him gently. He waited. The sounds had died away, but he still felt the subconscious stir caused by an aura outside his own.

"Who is there?"

He had intended to whisper, but his tongue had swollen and his voice came in a hoarse croak, startling even himself.

He listened while the blood hammered in his ears, but no reply came. He shifted his position a little and strove to relax so that the blood pressure would lessen and permit his hearing to function acutely once more. He strained his eyes until flashes of light came and went, but he knew what that meant.

"Imagination."

With the thought he allowed his mind to go back to Junius once more, but a few moments later he was again tense, listening as fresh sounds reached him. And this time he knew there could be no mistake. Someone was close to him, someone whose breathing was low, hurried, excited.

He thrilled as he felt a touch, a hand on his thigh. He waited. He could do nothing else. The hand was withdrawn but returned in a moment, this time in contact with his shoulder. And then a familiar scent was wafted into his nostrils, the strange exotic odour that he had always associated with only one person —Carlotta.

He felt a warm breath against his cheek; soft hair brushed his eyes; an arm lay across his chest, and then warm lips were close to his ear.

"Romair,"

It was Carlotta.

"Yes."

His lips moved, but he could not have told if the whisper escaped them. He was alert enough now that he was sure. But what had brought her here in this surreptitious manner, he was asking himself. Why had she crept in through the darkness? Where was Junius? What was her game this time?

"Romair, it is I, Carlotta. You hear?"

"Yes."

"You listen to me, Romair. Junius is verree angry with you. He is driving with Julia, so I come to see you. You were verree foolish to come this way. Junius knew you would come, and was ready. If you had been more careful and let me know, I could have helped. But maybee it is not too late. I help you now, Romair."

"I've had a sample of your help," grunted Walmsley, whose voice had come back suddenly. "I think I'll play a lone hand. I'm not forgetting how you and Junius tied me in a knot three years ago."

With a suddenness that took his breath away, her arm tightened across him, her lips crushed on his, her whole body smothered upon him. He squirmed irritably. The woman sensed his distaste and relaxed

"You are the big fool, Romair!" she panted. "I would have helped you three years ago, but you would not listen. Then Junius was strong, but now he is stronger. He is, oh, so cunning. I learn much in three years, Romair. But I forgive you and make you again the offer. We can go away, but it will be necessary to kill Junius, if he follows. There are many, many jewels. We can take them with us. You will come, Romair? You will not again refuse Carlotta? One little word, Romair, and I set you free. We go quickly before Junius returns, and then I show you verree great wealth."

"No."

She gripped him again, her fingers digging into his flesh until he flinched. In the uprush of her rage she forgot caution.

"You say me no again?" she demanded. "You not once more spurn Carlotta. I not offair twice. You refuse, and nevair again you see the light. I tell Junius."

"Tell him what you wish, you crooked little devil," returned

Walmsley. "I'm having no truck with you. I wouldn't trust you any farther than a fer de lance snake. Leave me alone —that's all I ask of you."

"I leave you alone, verree well," she trembled. "Oh, yais, I leave you alone. We see what Junius say. I tell him manee things and he kill you. You pig fool."

With that the infuriated woman drew away from him and crept through the darkness towards the secret entry by which she had come in. Walmsley was conscious of subdued sounds for a few moments, then silence.

But quickly again he was alert as fresh noises caught his ear. They were the same little scraping sounds he had heard some minutes before Carlotta's entry. He listened until they, too, died away and heavy silence reigned once more.

But he was certain he knew the meaning. Someone else had been in the cellar while Carlotta was there, had crept in before she came, had heard what passed between him and Carlotta, and now had gone in the same secret way.

Who had been spying?

Chapter 7.   The Two Crooks.

ON the morning after Romer Walmsley's rash visit, Junius Markheim motored to town.

He was fashionably dressed, but not too immaculate in a suit of light grey Saxony, with a soft white silk shirt, a black-and-white tie, in which nestled a lustrous pearl, a grey trilby hat and grey gloves— a well groomed, prosperous-looking man, bulk and all.

Sitting in the back of a big Daimler saloon he might have been taken for some rich City merchant, powerful executive, or captain of industry. He was the latter, but in the French sense, not the English.

If Junius Markheim had given any thought to Romer Walmsley since he had seen him vanish through the trap in the floor the previous afternoon, it had not prompted him to fare below and inquire as to the well-being of his prisoner. He had given certain orders which he considered sufficient for the present.

As a matter of fact, Markheim was well pleased with Walmsley's arrival, since the result had been so satisfactory. He had known for some time that Walmsley had escaped from prison in South America, and knew that eventually a reckoning must come. It was the one anxiety he had had while striving to secure himself through Julia de Santos' signature to certain papers —a consent he had strongly hoped to obtain during the drive the previous day.

But Julia had been as difficult as ever. At the first hint of the matter she had become vague though Markheim had believed for some time past that she was completely under the domination of his will. She was submissive enough; she was yielding, almost flaccid.

Yet he was still without that signature which would place him in safety. And it was essential, more than ever now that Walmsley had appeared, that he should get it. Had he not been so completely certain that no one within his own household could betray him, he would have begun to suspect that there was an influence opposed to his own in contact with the girl.

But that was impossible. There was only Carlotta and —the other. Neither would dare to intrigue against him. And his servants held him in too much fear. They were his creatures all of them. The other — the one who acted as dragon to Julia —

He pondered on this for a moment while the big saloon swung round Piccadilly Circus and headed into Regent Street. But when it drew into the kerb before one of the ultra-modern buildings which have sprung up there in the past two or three years, he shook his great shoulders with a hint of impatience. He need not fear her; she was the very last to betray him. Besides, all women were easily enough handled if one kept the whip hand, and Junius Markheim flattered himself he knew how to wield the knout.

When the chauffeur in grey livery opened the door Markheim picked up a small black portfolio and stepped out.

"One hour," was all he said.

In the marble-lined hall of the building he entered a lift that whisked him up to the fifth floor. A short distance down the wide, well-lighted hall he paused before a door that bore no name or designation of any sort. A thin yale key gave him entry to a sumptuously-furnished room. Depositing his hat and gloves, he seated himself at a wide mahogany desk, on the spotless blotting-pad of which had been placed a small pile of letters.

He began to open each envelope methodically. Of the lot only two seemed to hold his interest —one from a well-known Hatton Garden jewel dealer, the other from a gem broker in Paris..

When, he had finished the light task Markheim opened a drawer, in the desk and bundled the pile out of sight; then he reached out and touched a button. A tap came on a door which he faced as he sat, and a young man entered, murmuring an obsequious "Good-morning, sir!"

Markheim grunted something; then:

"There was an appointment at eleven o'clock."

"Yes, sir, the gentleman has just come in."

"You will wait one full minute, then bring him to me."

"Very good, sir."

The clerk withdrew, and Junius Markheim took up the small leather portfolio which had been lying at his elbow. Unlocking it, he drew out a roll of white velvet which he placed on the blotting-pad. Next he eased the right-hand top drawer a trifle so he could jerk it open swiftly if necessary, and, that done, helped himself to a cigar from a cedarwood box on the desk.

Scarcely had he taken the first testing puffs than a tap again came at the door, which swung open to admit a tall, swarthy man of about forty, with intensely black hair and moustache and beard of the same shade, the later clipped to a sharp point. He was dressed in regulation morning-coat and striped cashmere trousers, but their cut proclaimed the continental tailor rather than the English. He wore pince-nez, through the rather thick lenses of which a pair of piercing dark eyes fixed Junius Markheim. He carried a glossy silk hat, gloves and stick in his left hand, and, when the clerk had closed the door, he bowed formally.

Markheim evidently considered this visitor of sufficient importance to receive a certain consideration, for he rose and walked half the way to meet him.

"You are Monsieur Benoit?"

"At your service, Monsieur Markheim."

They shook hands, and Markheim relieved the other of his hat. Then he drew forward a desk armchair similar to the one he himself had been occupying, placing it so the visitor would be sitting vis-a-vis.

The two stared into each other's eyes for the space of about ten seconds, taking measure, as it were. And such measure each would need, for there weren't to be found two shrewder crooks in all Europe than Junius Markheim and Francois Benoit, though each believed the other honest. Markheim smiled his fat smile and pushed the box of cigars towards Benoit. But the latter shook his head.

"I will, with your permission, smoke one of my own cigarettes, monsieur."

He extracted a long, thin tube from a beautifully-chased gold cigarette-case and accepted a light from Markheim's lighter. Then he leaned back, his gaze passing briefly over the roll of white velvet that lay in front of Markheim.

"You have heard from Monsieur Acier?" he asked at last.

Junius Markheim had been born in England, but he was a citizen of all countries, and spoke a dozen different languages fluently. In a more honest if humbler sphere of life he could have done quite well as an instructor in a school of languages. He had "the ear," and now he tried to detect in his visitor's accent some hint of his true origin. He passed as a Frenchman, and might indeed be one, but his English was quite flawless. Markheim was baffled and inwardly irritated.

"I had a letter only this morning. He spoke of your presence in London, and hoped we had already met."

"He will know to-day that I am seeing you. I wrote him last night. Did he have anything special to communicate, monsieur?"

"No. He said you would handle matters."

"That is so. And now, the stones."

Junius Markheim laid podgy but very capable hands on the white velvet roll and untied the tapes that held it. Then he allowed it to flatten out, revealing, against the soft white sheen of the material, a collection of emeralds, uncut, but to the eye of knowledge of perfect colour.

He pushed the roll nearer his visitor and leaned back, watching. Benoit bent over the desk, shifted his position a little so the light fell more to his satisfaction, then put out a tentative finger and touched one of the stones.

He was unhurried in his examination, but from this stone to that he transferred his scrutiny in a way that told Markheim he knew his business. When he had rolled over the last of the dozen or so he made a little sound with his tongue and straightened up.

"A very fair sample, monsieur. Is it representative?"

"As I wrote you in Paris, yes."

"Are you prepared to state the approximate quantity?"

"Not until negotiations have advanced farther. But I will tell you this much— the quantity is sufficient to give control of the emerald market for some time to come. I speak of knowledge, and you are aware that emeralds are becoming the most fashionable of precious stones."

"True. But it has always been understood that the government of the republic of Colombia controls the output, aside from the unimportant quantity that comes from Australia. There would be no question of the title?"

Junius Markheim smiled slightly.

"I shall not pretend to misunderstand you, monsieur. There is nothing to fear on that score. I am not offering stolen goods. These stones were mined before the republic of Colombia came into existence. I do not care to say more at present, but I can assure you that the title is quite sound and the stones may be dealt in quite openly. It is a matter of indifference to me whether I dispose of them myself through the ordinary trade channels, or make a sale of the lot to you and your partner or some other dealers. I should prefer a single turnover, as I have other business on hand, and, as I said, the firm that holds the collection I have for disposal can dictate the price of emeralds for some time to come."

"And you ask for the lot, monsieur?"

"One million pounds."

"They are all open for inspection?"

"Any inspection and examination within reason; terms cash."

"There would be no delay? The collection is all in this country?"

"Every stone can be shown at twenty-four hours' notice."

"The price is high."

"Not high enough. There is half a million profit in the deal if one is patient enough to ease the stones on to the market a few at a time."

"You interest me, monsieur. Of course, you understand I must consult with my partner, M. Acier. But I am anxious to get the matter settled one way or another as soon as possible. I can get through by trunk telephone to him during the day. How soon could you arrange for a view of the whole collection?"

Junius Markheim did not answer at once. The point to which each man had been working was reached. It was something definite at last —the very thing that Markheim had been planning so carefully for months past. No man knew better than he the risks attendant upon trying to dispose of a whole chest of gems, a treasure trove such as one only read of in highly-imaginative stories of the pirate days of old, without rousing suspicion and unwelcome inquiry.

It was a different proposition entirely from getting rid of stolen gems through a "fence." It was a collection such as had not been brought to light for perhaps two hundred years with the exception of the Russian jewels that had been smuggled out of the Bolshevist chaos. And here a title would be demanded. He had stated confidently enough that he could deliver such title, a thing he did not possess nor would possess until Julia de Santos signed her name. But Junius Markheim was quite certain of securing that signature. Either she would give it, or her refusal would cost her her life.

"It is a matter of some delicacy, as you can understand," he said slowly at last. "I should have to be assured of complete secrecy whether we did business or not."

"I am prepared to give you any undertaking, monsieur."

"And submit to the conditions I should exact?"

"Assuredly."

"Then I suggest that you get through on the trunk telephone to M. Acier. I could get in touch with you later in the day and make a definite arrangement."

"That would be satisfactory. You could telephone to me at the Hotel Venetia where I am staying."

"At what time?"

"Any time after four."

"I shall do so."

The visitor rose and took his leave. No sooner had the door closed after him than Junius Markheim opened the right-hand drawer of the desk and, reaching in, pressed a button that had been fitted under the top of the desk. No response came from the outer room of his own offices, but in a room just opposite Markheim's suite a buzzer was set in motion.

In this room, very plainly furnished with a desk and a single chair, a man was sitting reading a newspaper. At the first sound of the buzzer he laid down the paper and rose, standing a good six feet as he reached for his hat. He was dressed in a blue serge suit, and, to the casual eye, would have appeared as a broker in a small way.

The critical glance, however, would have detected that indefinable something about him which had the stamp of an ex-policeman. And that conclusion would have been right, for ex-Detective-sergeant Cramer had left the Yard some two years before under a cloud, and, after a precarious career as a private inquiry agent, had become a unit in the machine controlled by Junius Markheim.

By the time the buzzer ceased he had reached down a bowler hat and umbrella, and, stepping out into the corridor, was just in time to see Markheim's late visitor emerge and make his way towards the lift.

Chapter 8. The Escape.

WALMSLEY had plenty of time in which to ponder on the coming and going of the mysterious eavesdropper.

The time that had elapsed from his pitching into the trap and the coming of Carlotta had seemed hours; but that period loomed as a brief span compared to the drag that followed her furious departure. Yet he guessed from what she had let drop that the discomfort of his position was causing his imagination to miscalculate badly. If Junius had been driving when she crept to him with her unwelcome proposal then it seemed reasonable to suppose that it was still late afternoon or, at most, early evening.

He would have felt gratitude even to Carlotta if she had offered him a draught of water. But for an age of time after the rustling departure of the unknown, he was left to suffer a growing torture of thirst.

It came to him that Junius might intend him to lie there until he died of starvation or thirst or both. Junius was quite capable of doing so. Indeed, it was a little difficult to understand why the drop through the trap hadn't been made deeper so as to ensure a broken neck to the one who became the victim. There was no doubt that the bullet that had struck him on entering the study had been intended for his heart and would have reached it, too, had it not been for the chain shirt he wore.

He had nothing that Junius could want. As long as he was alive and free he was a menace to Markheim and his plans; dead he would cease to be a problem. Therefore it seemed a perfectly reasonable supposition that since the fall through the trap had not killed him, Junius would find other means to effect his end.

The outlook was sufficiently disturbing on analysis to make him almost forget, for some time, the torture of his throat and the acute irritation of his bonds. But the throbbing and burning returned after that brief surcease with redoubled force and as his agony mounted to an almost unbearable pitch, Walmsley would have given up all claim to the treasure and determination for vengeance in exchange for one blessed draught of water.

Yet, even in the semi-deliriousness that seized him he knew that imagination had its limits. Time must be passing to some extent. He strove to discount the suggestion that arose from his condition and place a minimum on the period. Evening or night? Late evening, he decided, might be safe.

He tried to compose himself to clarity of thought but, despite his efforts, a drowsiness born of numbed senses seized upon him and he dropped into a fitful doze.

How long it lasted he had no idea. He struggled back to a realisation of his position to find himself blinking before a light. After no little difficulty in getting his eyes to focus he was able to trace the wired front of a cowled lantern, the slide of which had been opened just enough to make a pool of light where he lay. Behind the lantern and at each side, in the penumbra, he made out the vague forms of two persons.

While he still blinked in confusion, one of the forms moved within the full glare of the light. He saw an ill-favoured fellow with dark skin and oddly-set, oblique eyes. He needed no more than that for recognition. It was Jose, gutter sweeper of Santa Marta and one of the gang that had accompanied him and Markheim that fatal morning three years before.

Jose gave no sign of recognition. With a rough pull he dragged Walmsley away from the wall near which he lay and rolled him over. A few twists loosened his bonds and then Walmsley was hauled to a sitting posture. Then the fellow brought a knife into view, the point of which he held within a hairsbreadth of Walmsley's body. Had he pressed it closer he must have felt the metallic hardness of the chain shirt.

Half a loaf of bread and an earthenware jug of water were produced. Jose made an imperative motion with his free hand to indicate that the prisoner should eat and drink. Walmsley was not backward. His hands trembled as he grasped the jug and raised it. Nothing in all his life, not even the first breath of freedom after his escape from foul prison, had ever tasted so exquisite.

But wisdom of experience taught him caution. He drank as sparingly as possible, then forced himself to swallow chunks of the bread. With the resumption of normal functions his tongue and throat became less painful, though even to the last mouthful he had difficulty in swallowing. He finished off with another deep draught of water, rolling the liquid round and round his tongue in an ecstasy of pleasure.

Jose grabbed the jug away from him with a muttered curse.

Walmsley did not protest. Nor did he resist when they again bound his arms. Had he been left in possession of his gun and had his legs been free he would have made a fight of it; but with only his hands he knew such a course would only lead to more stringent restraint.

The one thing that did seem worth holding to at the moment was the thought that, after all, Markheim did not intend to leave him to die like a rat in a trap. Which meant, if it were so, that Junius either had some further devilry in mind or intended finishing him off at a more suitable time and place.

Walmsley would have given a good deal just then for a few puffs at his treasured briar, but he knew the futility of asking such a favour and lay resigned to the inevitable, while Jose and his companion withdrew. But just how they had entered and how they left he could not tell, for the lantern was dowsed before their departure. Still, Walmsley had seen enough to know that his original guess wasn't so far out of fact, for the place had appeared to be a cellar of some sort, lined with cheap planed deal boards.

From then on, Walmsley tried to keep a measured count of the passage of time. But again and again he found himself dozing off and, at last, yielded to the drowsiness that had followed the taking of the food. His wakings were intermittent and fitful, but how long each period of sleep endured he could not even make a vague guess. It might be hours that he lay unconscious, it might be merely minutes.

Gradually he became fatalistic. Junius would make another move when he was ready and not before. There was nothing to be gained by trying to anticipate. He had made a hash of the job and was utterly at Markheim's mercy. His only course was to sit tight and watch for a chance to turn the tables or escape.

It was a definite touch against his body that roused him from one of his spells of drowsiness. In a moment his mind was clear, his eyes wide open trying to pierce the gloom.

He knew instinctively that it was not Jose and his companion. Nor could it be Markheim. Junius would not come in that manner. Then came the thought of Carlotta. Had she returned? Had her anger cooled, and was she again ready to wheedle him with an offer?

He waited. The hand had been withdrawn but he could hear a faint scraping sound as of someone crawling along the floor. He was not wrong in his deduction. Something touched his shoulder and then a low hiss of caution reached his ear. A faint breath of some perfume drifted to his nostrils, but it was not the exotic scent which Carlotta affected. Yet he knew, somehow, the invisible intruder was a woman.

"Be quiet and do not speak."

The words were breathed in his ear.

"Who are you?" His whisper seemed extraordinarily loud in the confined stillness of the place.

"Never mind. Try and sit up —I will help you."

Walmsley obeyed, feeling hands hauling at his shoulders while he struggled to a sitting posture.

Then he was pushed aside a little and cold steel touched his wrists as a knife was drawn backwards and forwards against his bonds. He was wise enough to remain quiescent and wait for what followed. That came quickly. When the strands of cord fell away, he felt hands plucking at his ankles. Reaching out he touched an arm covered with what seemed a stiff shiny material. There was no doubt now about the sex of the invisible one.

"I can manage if you give me the knife," he whispered.

The unknown released the handle and Walmsley made short work of the cords. Then he again felt the nearness of the other and the uncertain groping of hands against his arm. A thrill went through him as his fingers came up and closed on the butt of a pistol that seemed familiar to his clutch.

"Get to your feet and come," was the command. "I have a few words to say before you go. It will not be easy for you to get away, but there is a chance. Can you walk?"

Walmsley signified that he could. She plucked his sleeve and led him through the darkness for a few paces. There was a pause, followed by a scraping sound, and then Walmsley was drawn along again, his feet stumbling over a low sill of sorts.

Once more he was brought to a halt while, he guessed, the door or panel was drawn back into place. Then on again, short footsteps of uncertainty as he kept close to his mysterious guide.

There came still another halt, and now the guide took his hand, guiding it upwards until he felt a wooden bar.

"Listen," he heard her whisper. "You go through that door. You have but to lift the bar and the way is clear. You will find a passage that leads into a cellar. There will be some light there. A door takes you to steps that lead to the open. Do you understand?"

"Yes; but who are you? Why do you do this?"

"You have been seeking Junius Markheim. You were a fool to come so openly. He has been ready and waiting for years. You must return in a different way. But you will never touch those jewels you seek unless you make a vow and keep it."

"I thought there was a nigger in the woodpile," said Walmsley to himself; but aloud: "What is the vow?"

"That you will not leave a second time without taking with you someone who must be got away from here. If you refuse or fail in that vow I shall see that you do not succeed in the other."

"Are you the person?"

There was a sniff of disdain.

"No; I could leave at any time. It is Julia de Santos."

"Ah! Then gossip did not lie!"

"You have heard me. Do you promise?"

"I promise."

"Then go. Time is short, for Junius Markheim is negotiating now to dispose of the treasure. He hasn't secured Julia de Santos' written consent, but he will get it. Go. If you are seen you will be fortunate to get clear of the grounds; if you are afraid, return to your prison."

Walmsley would have given a good deal to get a sight of the mysterious person who seemed to be so willing to betray Markheim. He knew it wasn't Carlotta, and he knew it could not be Julia de Santos. But beyond that he could not make a guess. Nor did he waste time now. All he wanted was to get into the grounds and take what chance offered.

"I'm off," he whispered. "I won't try to thank you, but you can take it I shall return —if I get away. Then I'll repay. Au revoir!"

She moved suddenly away and he lifted the bar. A faint patch of grey light some distance beyond gave him guidance. He drew the big door after him and heard the bar fall back into place. The woman was evidently going another way to reach the upper part of the house.

Walmsley found himself in the cellar she had indicated, a long, musty-smelling place with a low ceiling and a pile of broken coal just under a small window through which the light was filtering.

He spied the steps she had spoken of and mounted them, to find a door barring his progress. But it was unhooked and yielded readily enough to his pressure. Then he stepped out on to a gravelled path and, after a quick glance to right and left, realised he was at the back of the house, almost facing the stables.

Beyond the buildings was the stretch of park and, not caring to risk passing the front of the house, Walmsley started for the nearest turf. He did not know just how many of the type of Jose and his companion Markheim might keep about the place, but he remembered the woman's warning, and kept his fingers curled round the butt of the pistol which he had thrust into the right-hand pocket of his jacket.

He hadn't covered half a dozen steps before he had sharp proof that the warning had been no idle utterance, for, just as he cleared the corner of the big stable and was about to step on the turf, he heard a shout followed by the crack of a weapon, and a bullet kicked up the gravel at his feet.

Walmsley did not pause to return the shot. He broke into a run and ran as fast as his stiff limbs would allow in the direction where he thought to find the boundary of the estate.

TWO men plunged out of the nearer stable building, neither of which he saw in one fleeting glance, was Jose.

But from their swarthy skin he knew them to be of the same breed, and there was no doubt about their intention. Each was shooting as he ran at an angle that threatened to cut across Walmsley's course.

The fugitive swung sharply to the right, heading for the park-like stretch where great oaks and elms and beeches gave shade but no cover. Far in the distance he thought he could see the boundary wall which he had passed on his way down the valley.

A fusillade of shots that spattered dangerously close to his feet and clipped into the thick bark of an oak he was just passing, told him that danger was coming from another direction. He swung round the oak and jerked his own weapon into action.

Now he saw Jose and two more of his kind running round the corner of the house, and, at the same moment, another man with Carlotta appeared in the porch.

Walmsley shot twice, once towards Jose and once towards the pair that was coming from the stable. Luck or good aim was with him. To each bullet a man went down, and, turning, Walmsley raced on again, his last vision of Carlotta being a vivid crimson splash in the porch with the brilliantly-hued macaw flapping its wings and screaming invectives.

From the first moment of plunging into the open Walmsley regained conception of time. A blazing sun was climbing towards the zenith, marking the hour as between ten and noon. It seemed incredible to him that so many hours could have passed while he dozed fitfully in his prison hole, but there was no denying the morning and its promise.

If he could reach the road outside, if he could gain the valley, he would stand on more equal ground. He did not know if there were other habitations in the valley, but, daring though Markheim might be, it did not seem likely that he would risk inquiry by turning his gunmen loose on the countryside. As to Markheim's whereabouts Walmsley didn't have time just then to wonder or care.

From the oak tree that had given him momentary cover he took a zig-zag course towards a tall, leafy beech. His limbs were free enough now, and Walmsley had always been able to show a good turn of speed. He needed it. The man left from the pair that had burst from the stable was loping towards him in the rangy way that marked the seasoned, long-distance runner, and Walmsley had been in Colombia long enough to know that the descendants of the old Indian trail-makers had inherited both stamina and speed.

He reached the beech and took two more snapshots, missing with both. Jose had stopped and was firing steadily; his remaining companion was keeping straight on. Walmsley risked Jose's aim, stepped out from cover and shot deliberately. The nearest pursuer stumbled and pitched on to his face.

Walmsley flung round and began his zig-zag course again. Came a beech round which he swung to dart at an angle towards an elm. He reached it and raced for another elm from which he darted to the cover of an enormous oak.

Ahead of him now was the brick and flint boundary wall, plainly visible. Jose and the fellow on the left had joined forces but had stopped shooting. Yet Walmsley did not discard the zig-zag strategy he had adopted. From tree to tree he raced, holding his own precious ammunition now, and concentrating on just one thing, to reach the wall.

Suddenly, just head of him in a dip in the ground, he saw a low, thick hedge forming a rough, circular enclosure. Walmsley made for it, skirting it until he came to an opening. He darted in, and then would have drawn up, for he found himself on the verge of a steep bank that ran down to a patch of stagnant water.

But his feet had already begun to slip, and, finding it impossible to stop, he let himself go, plunging in to his armpits with soft mud dragging at his ankles.

Cursing, he scrambled back to the edge, tried to clamber out, failed to hold on and slid back. He turned and cast a quick glance about him. At one end the bank sloped more gradually. If he could reach that before Jose and his companion came through the opening —

He stumbled along, his feet held in strong suction by the mud. It was as if he were weighted in glue so reluctantly did the sticky clay release him. So intent was he on reaching his objective that he gave no attention to the details of his passage. It was not until he found himself entangled in a patch of water-lily stalks that he realised the peril of this new handicap.

He knew only too well the danger of fighting against the insidious hold of the stalks. He felt the inevitable rush of panic as they wound about his ankles and legs, seeming to rotate and cling with each movement of the water. He kept his head, and disregarding pursuit for the moment, thrust his weapon inside his coat and bent down, thrusting his arms under water so he could grip the smooth stems.

He dragged and hauled with all his strength. One or two of the stalks broke away, but the main bunch had become so entangled within itself that he could not exert strength enough to tear the mass away from the parent root.

He stood up and listened. Voices drifted to him from some little distance away, and he knew that Jose and his companion could not have seen his sudden disappearance into the circle of screening bushes. But it would not be long before they picked up the trail. As soon as they found he had not made the wall and gone over they would soon pitch on the enclosure.

Once more he bent down, and working gently, endeavoured to work the clinging stalks away from his ankles. It was while he was thus engaged that he looked along the surface of the water and noticed a small patch of water-reeds, not indigenous to the country, he knew, but a decorative water-plant imported at some time or other by a previous owner of the place.

It was here that Walmsley's jungle training was to stand him in good stead. With a sudden idea in his mind he gripped the remaining stalks and heaved with all his strength. They clung tenaciously, but when it seemed that he must let go he felt a slight yielding. Little by little the mass came away until the remaining tentacles gave as one. Walmsley pitched backwards with the unexpected release of the obstacle and flopped loudly into the water.

He recovered swiftly, spitting muddy water from his mouth. That the noise of his plunge had been heard and had roused suspicion he knew a few moments later when he heard voices calling and growing nearer as they called.

He reached the shallow water near the bank and waded along to the patch of water-reeds. A brief examination showed him they were hollow and fairly brittle. He turned towards the sound of the voices, and now could hear Jose shouting to the other to join him. The mestizo was obviously heading straight for the enclosure of bushes.

Walmsley waited for no more. Reaching down as far as possible he broke off a long reed and drew it clear of the surface. Once more he broke the end until it revealed a clean hole, then he served the top end in similar fashion, having left in his hand a hollow reed about four feet long.

A voice just on the other side of the bushes sent him into precipitate action. Down into the water he went, one hand reaching for the lower tangle of the reeds so that he might hold himself down; the other pushed the reed stalk up so that the upper end was above the surface close to its unbroken companions, the lower between his lips. Then he dragged himself close to the anchorage of the bed and lay as still as possible, using his hollow reed as a breathing-tube.

Up above him the water showed in a disturbed patch where he had been, and back among the lily-stalks, the mud had been churned up; ripples were still making bankwards when Jose lurched through the opening and stood gazing over the stagnant expanse. But Walmsley could not hear what was said.

Time passed. The difficulty to inhale and exhale through the narrow tube almost forced the hidden man to let go and rise to the surface time and again. But he knew what fate awaited him the moment his head showed above water if the two mestizos discovered him. He hung on grimly, striving to hold the tube steady, endeavouring that no bubbles should rise from the corners of his mouth to betray him.

But his limit of endurance was reached. Death or no, he must break surface. Slowly he eased himself upwards, still clinging to the reeds until his head came above water. Opening his eyes, he peered cautiously about him.

He shook his head to get rid of the water that filled his ears. Then he heard voices once more, but whether his pursuers had been within the enclosure or not he could not tell.

He waited, but they seemed to grow farther away. He waited longer until he could hear them no more. Then, cautiously, he waded to the bank and scrambled to the top.

He stood listening. Just then not a sound seemed to break the stillness of the lovely summer morning. Even the face of the stagnant pool preened itself to a sheen of loveliness as a slanting ray of sun found it out.

It was a stillness that made Walmsley uneasy, yet he told himself he must have thrown Jose and his fellow off the track. He moved along with infinite precaution towards the opening through which he had come. Peering out, he gazed across the park. Not a soul met his view. But beyond was the house, and while that lay so close there was danger.

He crept out and rounded the bushes. Following the curve of the line he kept on until once more he caught sight of the boundary wall. It stood perhaps forty yards away. This time he must reach it.

He broke from the shelter of the bushes and began to run. As he did so a bloodcurdling scream sounded almost directly over his head. Involuntarily, he drew up and gazed into the branches of a giant oak. Again that harsh scream broke on his ears, followed by a noisy flapping, and then a flash of purple and scarlet whirred out of the leafy cover as the macaw darted towards him.

Straight towards his throat the bird winged, its scimitar-like beak ready to cut a sweeping gash in the flesh. The hatred that Walmsley had always felt for the creature welled up within him in such profound force as to demand expression even at the risk of betraying his whereabouts.

Jerking up his weapon he fired at the bird just as it circled within two yards of his head. The macaw jeered and screamed in a perfect frenzy of rage and excitement, swooped this way and that until Walmsley grew dizzy with trying to follow its erratic course; then he found himself clawing wildly at a bundle of feathered devilry as the macaw made vicious efforts to reach his throat.

He drove the creature off and shot again as it winged, jeering, towards the cover of the big oak. Then he was recalled to his own precarious situation as another weapon sounded in the near distance and a bullet whistled past his ear.

He turned, saw Jose and the other mestizo racing across the park from the direction of the house. He shot twice, pulled trigger a third time on an empty gun, then waiting no longer he dashed for the wall, the macaw winging once more after him as it gave vent to fiendish invectives that rose to a pitch of uncontrollable fury.

Chapter 10. The Fugitive.

THE wall presented a difficulty of height.

It was fully ten feet high and offered no projection for hands or feet. Checked, Walmsley looked desperately to right and left. Shouts and a patter of bullets against the brick warned him that his pursuers were getting closer. Over his shoulder he saw that Jose had brought reinforcements with him, for fully half a dozen men were running in a straggling line towards him. Had there been only the two who had driven him to cover in the pool he would have fought it out. But the odds of six to one were too great.

About ten yards to his left was a low branching oak with one great limb that reached almost to the top of the wall. Low irregularities in the trunk would offer some sort of foothold for a spring upwards.

Walmsley raced for this new goal, and while still on the move, used his impetus for the spring. His hands caught the limb, slipped and held. With dangling legs scraping for purchase against the rough trunk he managed to cling at last and draw himself up. It was a miracle that one of the bullets that followed him did not reach the mark, for the flying lead was chipping off the rough bark all about him.

Sprawling along the branch like a nightjar he got his balance and began crawling. Halfway to the wall he found that he could reach another limb above by standing, and thus assisted, he moved more rapidly towards the end that bent lower and lower under his weight.

Jose was more than dangerously close. He and another of the gang were almost under the tree when Walmsley let go with his hands, and allowing the branch on which he stood to take his full weight, watched his chance as it dipped.

He sprang, and landed on the top of the wall. Swaying there, he was a target for further shots, but it was not a bullet that reached him. A knife, thrown with perfect accuracy, ripped through the sleeve of his jacket, hung for a moment, then fell with a clatter to the hard ground outside the wall.

Walmsley allowed himself to fall to the right. His hands caught the top of the wall even as his body went over, and then, after one terrific jerk as his arms took the full weight, he let go. He landed in a sprawling heap, scrambled to his feet and broke into a run, his next

48

objective being the little stone bridge which he had crossed on his way to the main gates.

Before he had gone a score of yards someone began shooting from the top of the wall. Looking back, the fugitive saw two figures clinging to the narrow perch and the head and shoulders of a third just appearing into view.

While he ran he managed to get out a spare loaded clip which he had in his hip pocket. There was plenty of ammunition in the haversack which he had been forced to abandon, but there was no hope now of retrieving that.

By the time he was opposite the gates he had thrown away the empty clip and inserted the new. A quick back-pull threw a cartridge into the breech. He had slowed a little to perform this operation, but now, as he quickened his pace, he saw two swarthy men dash out from the lodge.

Walmsley took a snap shot at the one in front. The fellow gave a yell and wheeled quickly. He raced back the way he had come, while his companion drew up, paused and then, drawing back his arm, threw a knife at the oncoming fugitive.

Walmsley was already zig-zagging, and, on the throw, changed course with a quick side-swing. The knife whistled past him, but its clatter to the road was echoed by a further fusillade from the wall behind. The man by the gate was running towards the lodge when Walmsley fired again. This bullet missed, but a second brought him down.

The first fellow reappeared with a gun and drew a bead on Walmsley. The latter swung to the left, plunged headlong into some brambles, rolling through them with one arm across his eyes, and fetched up in a grassy strip beside the little stream.

He took to the water and reached the other side. Here he turned to the left, but at an angle that would take him up the bank to the road he had originally followed into the valley.

The firing behind ceased. Panting heavily, he drew up and looked back. Just as he did so he heard the rattle of a motor engine and saw one of the big gates swing inwards. Through the opening came a motor-cycle driven by another of the gang. Just outside he stopped and waited.

Turning his head, Walmsley saw Jose running at top speed towards the vehicle. Instead of continuing up the slope to the road,

Walmsley made in the direction of the stone bridge. He was still some ten yards away when Jose swung himself on to the pillion and the machine started with a roar.

Behind it trailed half a dozen or so of the gang; but these the fugitive disregarded. Jose was his meat. He had seen an open stretch at the end of the bridge which the machine must pass, and on this he drew a bead.

The motor-cycle was moving at a rising thirty by the time it struck the patch, but as it flashed past Walmsley fired twice in rapid succession. He did not aim at either of the men; his target was the machine itself. And he scored.

There was the sound of an explosion, the machine swerved violently, disappeared for a moment from Walmsley's view, reappeared close to the low stone parapet which it struck with terrific force, and then literally climbed the wall until it shot over the top, the engine racing and the wheels buzzing in mad gyration.

Jose had either been thrown off or had slid to safety; the man in the saddle still clung to his mount, and was astride when it struck the shallow water.

Walmsley saw only the crash. He did not wait for what might follow. He was racing back down the valley by the time Jose limped to the parapet and peered over at the wreckage in which the driver was lying entangled.

Across the open patch came the string of followers. They would have paused, but Jose screamed at them to go after Walmsley, his voice reaching the fugitive as he panted and puffed up a steep rise and plunged under a low rail to the road.

His pace was laboured, his heart hammering like a mad thing as he forced himself into a trot. The dust rose in little whorls as he ran, rising to his lips and filming his tongue. The heat beat up at him in shimmering waves; the sun burned with an ardent caress that scorched him. Still he forced himself on at a shambling run. There is no greater spur than the fear of death; and Romer Walmsley had more desire to live now than twenty-four hours before.

On turning a bend, he saw, not far ahead, the spot where he had paused the previous day to survey the valley. Beyond that lay the main road, and there was safety, for he remembered the farmhouse he had seen just before turning into the valley.

At the crest of the rise he drew up and turned, surveying the valley while he drank in great gulps of air to ease his tortured lungs. He could see dark forms on the bridge and near the gates; but no one appeared on the road. Several hundred yards were shut off from his view by the bend he had just negotiated, and Jose might be on the stretch.

But his position now gave him a certain vantage, and he held it while his breathing grew less laboured and his heart eased its wild pace. No one came into sight. Instead, more figures appeared on the bridge and he guessed that Jose, not willing to carry a running battle into the main road, had given up the chase. How he would explain matters to Markheim, Walmsley didn't know or care.

He began to walk at a brisk pace, turning every few moments to see if pursuit appeared round the bend. But not a stray shot followed him from there to the main road, and once he reached the tarred surface Walmsley breathed easier.

"That was a close shave," he confided to his briar as he pulled it out, "a very I close call indeed. The mystery to me is Junius. Where is he? If he had been in the house he would have led the attack. He must be off on some errand. And the woman who gave me the chance — who the deuce is she? And what sort of a tale will she pitch Junius when he returns? As for Carlotta —well, it wasn't she, but I wish I had got that cursed bird. There'll be some fireworks there when Junius turns up, or I don't know Junius. But if I am to return before he makes a move to checkmate me I've got to hustle. Julia de Santos — so she did come to England with him. And if the mysterious woman in black spoke the truth, then she must be a prisoner. Julia de Santos and the loot; can I swing it?"

He strode on until he came to a field gate, inside which were two stacks of hay. Unlatching the gate, Walmsley entered and passed behind one of the stacks. His face that had been puckered with anxiety cleared as he saw a heap of loose hay forming a flattish bulge against the side of the stack.

Catching hold of it he dragged it away, revealing as he did a twin-cylinder motor-cycle.

"I shouldn't have been surprised if it had been sneaked," he muttered. "If anyone had known, but it was a good gamble."

While he muttered he was removing what hay remained about it and, finishing, he was just on the point of wheeling it to the road when the low hum of a motor reached his ears. He crouched, peering round the end of the stack towards the gate. Nearer came the sound of the car, and then it flashed by, but not so quickly that Walmsley could not see the grey-clad figure of Junius Markheim in the back.

He waited only until the sound died away before pushing the machine into the road. Then, closing the gate, he kicked the starter and flung his leg over the saddle. Next moment he was dashing towards London in a cloud of dust.

•　　•　　•　　•　　•

Back in the house from which Walmsley had just escaped Carlotta and the woman in black stood face to face. They had met just as Carlotta turned back when the chase passed out of the grounds. At sight of the other she drew up, and a slow, meaning smile gave sinister threat to the words she uttered.

"So it was you who tampered with the prisoner. You will find it difficult to explain to Junius when he returns."

The grim-faced woman who faced her stood immobile, her hands folded across the stiff black silk gown.

"My explanation will be easy. But yours —how will you tell him you went to him in the dark and offered to betray Junius just as you tried to play him false three years ago?"

Carlotta drew back, pale under the cold accusation which she could not deny.

"That's —that's not true," she broke out hysterically.

"Don't lie to me. I was there and heard every word. Think of that and then decide what you will say to Junius."

And, disdaining further words, the woman in black walked slowly up the flight of black oak stairs, with an assurance of movement that caused the watching Carlotta's eyes to burn with a terrible hate.

There were undercurrents in Junius Markheim's house of which he knew nothing —as yet; undercurrents that were forming a dangerous whirlpool.

Chapter 11. Cards Down.

"YOU were right, Mr. Blake; I have been a fool!"

The detective glanced at his visitor quizzically.

"I can't answer for that, Mr. Walmsley. But you certainly seem to have been having a rough passage."

"I'll say I have. Will you listen to what I have to say?"

"If it is about this man Junius Markheim, isn't it rather a waste of time, Mr. Walmsley? I think we settled that subject when you were here a few days ago."

"I haven't come in the same way, Mr. Blake. I wish I had listened to your advice then. I see now what you meant. But I was so set on getting my own back that I went right ahead. And I must say Junius was more than ready for me."

"Mr. Markheim is a gentleman of many resources," remarked the detective casually.

Walmsley looked at him in surprise.

"You speak as if you knew something about him."

"I have discovered a little since you were here. I could tell you something about his professed business, and inform you where he lives, only it wouldn't be necessary. Unless I am greatly mistaken, you have discovered that for yourself, and received a warm welcome."

"True enough, as you shall learn. But tell me —how did you find out those things?"

"My organisation," drawled Blake. "My young man in the corner there made a few inquiries just so we should have the data. While I could not take your case, I was sufficiently interested in what you told me to wish to have a few particulars of Junius Markheim. One never knows when odd bits of information may come in useful. But suppose you tell me what has happened."

Walmsley needed no urging. In fact, all the way up from Sussex he had been telling himself that he could no longer play a lone hand against Markheim's defences. Nor was he anxious to disclose anything to the police. He had decided to lay all the facts before the detective. He would put all his cards on the table.

Curiously enough, the predominating idea in his mind was no longer the emeralds. As each mile had been reeled off that ambition seemed to lessen in force, giving place to a new aim that amazed him.

For Romer Walmsley had never been troubled by altruism.

Yet those few whispered words from the mysterious woman who had given him release had given birth to a new idea, a fresh ambition that he found was obliterating all selfishness. He had been sickened at the unnecessary and brutal killing of Don Edouardo de Santos, but it had not roused in him any particular desire to act as protector to the girl.

He had remembered her as a pretty little thing crying out in horror at her father's fate. But when he heard that she had accompanied Markheim and Carlotta out of the country he had dismissed her from his mind as a factor of no importance.

But now he visualised her as something helpless that needed him. He did not realise that it was Sexton Blake's remark that had opened his mind to the reception of his new idea. It had been ready laid even as he lay bound in the darkness at the house in Sussex; it had needed but those whispered words to ignite it into something almost noble. Hence his self-condemnatory words on this, his second visit to the detective.

Blake listened to the relation in silence. But that did not mean he was not interested. On the contrary. He realised even better than Walmsley that a metamorphosis was beginning to take place, though he by no means attempted to justify Walmsley's share in the shooting that had taken place at Markheim's place.

"I can't quite explain, Mr. Blake," he said hesitatingly when he had reached the point where, as he was about to wheel his motor-cycle out from behind the stack, he saw Markheim pass. "It's different somehow. I want to get at Markheim as badly as ever, but I don't want anything for myself now. I've got a hunch that there has been some hanky-panky in connection with Miss de Santos. I shall not be able to rest until I get her out of Markheim's clutches."

"Did you see her at all?"

"Not a sign. All I know is what the mysterious woman told me."

"Can you identify that woman?"

Walmsley did not answer at once. He was remembering that there had been a vague, shadowy personality in the background three years ago in South America— someone to whom Markheim seemed to yield a consideration so prompt that one might almost have believed he was inspired through fear if one hadn't found it difficult to associate such a thing with him.

He had mentioned the subject to Carlotta more than once, but each time she had blazed out in such fury that he had desisted. Not once had he actually laid eyes on her, but again and again he had felt the influence of her mysterious personality.

Something had warned him not to speak to Junius about it. So he had put the matter from his mind, and, in the stress of what followed, had given it no more thought until the strange visit in the secret room where he lay bound.

He explained as much to Blake.

"I can't quite place her," he added. "She doesn't strike me as the 'crook' type, but one never knows. She may be some flame of Markheim's, or an old associate who had her hooks into him. He must have hitched up with some weird birds in his time, and it is just possible he didn't always shed them as easily as he thought."

"It is someone who is so sure of her position that she dared to release you," rejoined the detective thoughtfully.

"I have a suspicion she was in the room when Carlotta came to me and made her offer to double-cross Markheim. There were some strange sounds which I couldn't place. They were audible just before Carlotta crept in, and I heard them again for a few moments just after she went. And she seems to be in close touch with Miss de Santos. But I know it wasn't she."

"No. Had it been Miss de Santos she would have made an attempt to go away with you if she were trying to escape. It seems to me that this fellow Markheim is running a very peculiar menage down in Sussex. He may have cut capers in South America, but if he has done anything crooked since he arrived in England he has kept it covered up very successfully, for there isn't a whisper against him at Scotland Yard. He has offices in Regent Street, and operates in a mild way on the Stock Exchange. Also he has been doing a little dealing in —emeralds. That is the one thing that can be chalked up against him, and it would be impossible to think anything wrong about that unless one were possessed of the information you have given me about the De Santos treasure."

Walmsley stared at the detective.

"I should say you have been making a few inquiries," he blurted. "You know a darned sight more about what he has been up to since he came to England than I have found out. But that only strengthens my case, Mr. Blake. I want your help. I feel that you know all the ropes.

And I give you my word of honour I shall be satisfied just to rescue Miss de Santos and lay Markheim by the heels in an orthodox way if you will help me. I ask nothing for myself. And I'll foot the bill. I'm not asking you to condone that killing of Don Edouardo. Think of the girl. It looks as if she were an unwilling guest in that house."

Before Sexton Blake could reply the telephone rang. Excusing himself, he drew the desk instrument nearer and lifted off the receiver. Had he possessed less control over his facial muscles Walmsley might have seen a sudden change in his expression as he listened to what was being said at the other end of the wire. But his immobile countenance yielded nothing, and his words told little more.

Yet he was no little astonished at what he heard, for the speaker was Detective-inspector Thomas of Scotland Yard, and he was asking what Blake could tell him about a French jewel crook of the name of Benoit.

"His record is one of the worst," was Blake's reply. "I don't suppose there is a smoother criminal in that particular line in all Europe. I am surprised that you know nothing of him."

"I know something about him all right!" grunted Thomas. "But it is some time since he came to my notice. I was wondering if you had anything recent."

"Not a thing. What is up?"

"He is in London, and we had the tip to pick him up. I put Lethbridge on the job, and he froze to him the moment he stepped off the train at Victoria. He must be on some game over here."

"Then it is a new stunt. I don't know that he has ever worked anything in this country. Perhaps it got too hot in Paris."

"We'll jump him as soon as he makes a break. But that isn't all I want to ask. Do you know anything about a fellow of the name of Markheim —Junius Markheim? He seems to have some offices in Regent Street, but I can't seem to find out much about him."

"I've heard of him," admitted Blake cautiously.

"Know anything against him?"

"I'm hardly at liberty to say just now. Why do you ask?"

"Because Lethbridge trailed Benoit to his offices. I just had a 'phone message in from one of Lethbridge's scouts. He is following Benoit now. I'm anxious to know more about this man Markheim, and what Benoit's business could be with him. Why are you so close-mouthed about it?"

"I'm not. I only said I did not feel at liberty to say much at the moment. But if you care to see me, I am willing to talk after I have discussed the matter with someone else."

"You mean you have to get permission?"

"That's it."

"Well, listen! Be a sport, Blake, and give Lethbridge a tip, if you can. I've got to go down to Birmingham on some business that may keep me out of town for some days. I'm leaving everything in Lethbridge's hands. I'll tell him to get in touch with you."

And before Blake could either accede to the request or refuse the inspector hung up.

Blake did the same, and turned back to Walmsley.

"That was from Scotland Yard," he said casually. "It was an inquiry for anything I might know about Junius Markheim."

Walmsley sat up with a jerk.

"What!"

"Just what I say. It seems that a certain well-known French jewel crook has arrived in London, and called on Junius Markheim this morning. Scotland Yard was tipped off by the Paris police, and this fellow had been shadowed from the moment he stepped off the train. When one remembers that Junius Markheim is in possession of a chest of emeralds of great value, one begins to wonder just why a high-flying crook like this Frenchman should visit him. My information goes to show that the emeralds of which Markheim has disposed so far have been through perfectly reputable dealers. But there you are. At this moment Benoit, the French crook, is being shadowed, and the instant he makes a break Scotland Yard will gather him in. In the circumstances, Mr. Walmsley, don't you think you might be wise to lay your case before Scotland Yard? Otherwise there might be a very nasty backwash if Markheim is netted along with Benoit."

"I'll do exactly what you suggest, Mr. Blake, if you will help me to my own ends."

"I am inclined to say 'yes' to that," rejoined Blake. "Suppose we get things down on paper, and then I shall get through to Inspector Lethbridge and make an appointment."

And Walmsley agreed, realising that from this moment it were safer that the direction of his affairs in so far as they touched on Junius Markheim and Julia de Santos should be in Blake's hands.

EX-DETECTIVE-SERGEANT CRAMER had, as has been said, left the Yard under a cloud. In a certain inquiry he had stoutly maintained his innocence of being connected with the irregularities which were the subject of the examination, and it is true that his participation had been no more than passive.

Out of a mistaken sense of loyalty to colleagues who were involved in the unsavoury business he had kept silence when he should have spoken. He had suffered no more than a reprimand and a reduction in rank. The first he could accept; the second was too much for his spirit. Had he been a strong character he would have gritted his teeth and fought his way back. But he was not of that calibre, and hence, some two years after returning to civilian life, he was to be found attached to Junius Markheim's wagon.

During the period he had attempted to carry on as a private inquiry agent he had been offered many a valuable tip by his old friends at the Yard, and had not a false pride kept him away from them and turned him surly he might have built up a very prosperous little business.

But he allowed his sense of an injustice done to overshadow everything else; his sense of values became warped; his thinking got muddled. The result was inevitable, and when, after an unimportant job for Markheim the latter had offered him a regular retainer with a room in the building in Regent Street, Cramer had accepted. It was a definite downward step, but he didn't regard it as such.

During his years as a police official Cramer had acquired a very sound technique along many lines of criminal investigation. One phase in particular he had developed to a fine art —that was the shadowing of a subject. He had an uncanny way of following his man for hours on end without rousing suspicion, and more than that had an instinctive flair for discovering if his own footsteps were being dogged.

This faculty stood him in good stead on the morning he left the building in Regent Street on the heels of Markheim's visitor, Monsieur Benoit. It was perfectly easy to follow his quarry at the beginning, for he walked leisurely along towards Piccadilly Circus, pausing now and then to survey the contents of a shop window that caught his fancy.

Cramer professed to be interested in another display at the same time, and thus their respective positions were maintained at more or less the same distance until they came opposite the Regent Street entrance to the Hotel Venetia.

It was then that Cramer became aware that he was being followed. Keeping one eye on Benoit he performed a simple manoeuvre to make sure if his suspicions were correct, and then he turned and walked back swiftly towards a tall, slim man who was idling along as if he were out only to enjoy the freshness of the lovely summer day.

Cramer wheeled again, and fell into step beside him.

"Well, Lethbridge, what is your game?" he asked gratingly. "Are you trailing me?"

Frank Lethbridge, Detective-inspector at Scotland Yard, smiled faintly. Two years before he and Cramer had been close friends, and after the latter's departure it had been Lethbridge who had stirred himself more than anyone else to help his erstwhile comrade. He knew that Cramer had been victimised through his own weakness, and he felt sorry that he had not had the moral courage to remain and face down the sneers and side glances that would be his portion while he rehabilitated himself.

"Partly you, but mostly your quarry, George," he murmured. "I'm wondering what interest you have in his nibs just ahead."

"What's that to you?"

"I don't want to spoil any private stunt of yours, George, but it is my job to learn a little more than we know about that bird ahead. And, by the same token, unless we are to lose him we'd better look nippy. He is hailing a taxi."

Cramer held up his hand to a cab that was coming towards them. He and the man from the Yard stepped in, Lethbridge leaving it to Cramer to give his instructions. When the taxi had turned and was following the one taken by Benoit, Lethbridge turned and looked at his companion.

"Do you know anything about this fellow, George?"

"No; never saw him before in my life."

"Then why were you trailing him out of that building?"

"That's my business."

"I dare say; but it is liable to have a sting to it. It happens to be my business as well. I don't suppose you care to tell me what he was doing in confab with your boss, Junius Markheim.''

Cramer shot him a look of surprise.

"How did you know I was working for him?"

"I didn't until this morning. You can believe it or not, George, but I'm not the only one at the Yard who wants to see you make good. But you're on a ticklish wicket with this man Markheim and — Benoit.''

"Markheim is on the level. Who is Benoit?''

"Our friend in the taxi ahead. Do you know that Benoit is one of the smoothest jewel crooks in Europe? We were tipped off by the Paris people that he was on his way to London. I was lucky enough to spot him as soon as he stepped out of the train at Victoria, and I've been watching him ever since. And I know he has been with Junius Markheim this morning. Birds of a feather, you say. That is why I am curious to learn what his business was with your boss. And I'll tell you something else, George, though I must ask you to treat it as confidential. I don't think I am making a mistake. I don't want to see you nipped in something serious, old man.''

"What is it?''

"We had an inquiry about Markheim at the Yard three days ago. Until then we didn't know he existed. We put out a few feelers, but couldn't locate him; didn't know where he hung out until this morning. It was Benoit that led me straight to him. I followed Benoit from the Hotel Venetia and watched him into the building. It didn't take me long to find out what room he had entered, and then to learn the name of the tenant of that suite. That was how I stumbled on Markheim. Think it over, George. Hallo! Shaftesbury Avenue! I wonder where our man is heading?''

Cramer was silent. Lethbridge's words worried him. Until that moment he had not had a grain of suspicion against Markheim. He had regarded him simply as a rich man who played a dilettante game on the Stock Exchange, and did a little trading in precious stones more as a connoisseur than anything else.

Markheim himself had hinted as much, and in taking him on his pay-roll had let it be understood that he wanted him more as a personal bodyguard than for any other purpose. He professed to be nervous about his safety when in possession of stones of value, and Cramer had believed him. More than that, during the three months or so he had been on the job, he had seen nothing to rouse his suspicions in any of the duties Markheim had given him. Mostly he just remained in the room that had been allotted to him, and on half a dozen different occasions he had trailed visitors from the building, finding mostly that they were jewel dealers from Hatton Garden. He did not know that Junius Markheim had been gradually testing him out in preparation for the day when he might find it necessary to issue far different orders.

Cramer saw the taxi ahead turn out of Shaftesbury Avenue into the Soho district; not until then did he respond to the conversation his companion had been making.

"That bird we are following may be a crook, but Markheim is all right," he said slowly. "What are you going to do, Frank?"

"Keep tabs on Benoit. He hasn't come across to London to study the pictures at Burlington House. He's up to some mischief, take it from me. And, look here, don't you think it's kind of funny that he should make tracks for your man, Markheim, as soon as he gets here?"

"He may be trying to pull some swindle on Markheim."

"Possibly. But don't forget what I said —birds of a feather. You take my advice and stand out from under, George, before something hits you on the snout. I'm your friend whether you want me as one or not, and I'd like to see you make good. I know you were one of the goats in that business two years ago."

"Markheim's my boss, and I'm not going to let him down," responded Cramer doggedly.

"All right, it's your funeral. But what I've said to you this morning is on the q.t."

"Don't you worry, I'm not going to spill anything, Frank."

"Then we'll stick together until we find out what this French crook is up to."

It was easy enough to keep the other taxi in sight through the narrow streets of Soho, and when the chase led along Old Compton Street, into Greek Street and thence to a narrow alley, Lethbridge tapped on the window for the driver to stop in Greek Street.

The two detectives got out and walked to the comer. Some little distance down the other taxi had drawn up in front of a small hotel that both Cramer and Lethbridge knew to have an unsavoury reputation. There was a dingy restaurant on the ground floor which was the haunt of shady characters.

Their quarry must have nipped out of the cab and crossed the pavement before they reached the corner, for the taxi began to turn round, and, passing them a few moments later, revealed no passenger inside.

"I guess that marks Benoit all right," said Lethbridge shortly. "He stays at the Venetia, but he seems to have business in that joint of Tony Costello's. We'll give him a few minutes, then have a word with Tony."

They stood on the corner talking as if they had just met in passing. During this time two negroes and three white girls passed and entered the hotel, not in a group, but singly. With the disappearance of the third white girl Lethbridge threw away his cigarette and glanced towards Cramer.

"Coming?"

"I'd better wait here and watch if he comes out while you are with Tony. I'm sticking on this job, Frank, and I'm doing a lot of thinking."

Lethbridge nodded, and started along. Cramer watched him disappear into the hotel; then, lighting a cigarette, he began pacing to and fro. Just what his thoughts were only he himself knew, but when he saw Lethbridge reappear he paused, and muttered:

"Frank may be right. It is darned queer why this French bird should hunt up Markheim as soon as he gets to London, and then hoof it for Tony Costello's dump immediately after his confab with the boss. I am not going to double-cross Markheim, but maybe I'd better pull out while there's a chance."

Just then the man from Scotland Yard joined him.

"Well?"

"He's up in one of the bed-rooms with a man who arrived at Tony's this morning— name of Acier, and signs from Paris. Probably he's a confederate of Benoit's. I'm going to put a man down here to keep an eye on the other one. What are you going to do, George?"

"I'll report to Markheim."

"Listen, man. If you did something on this job that made an impression at the Yard it might give you an opening to go back. I'm not saying anything definite, but I know the commish was sorry when you went. Think it over, old man. I'll put in my word, as you know. I've got a hunch that this Benoit may be trying to pull something big. We haven't got the strength of Markheim yet, but it looks queer.

Think it over, as I say. I'm going to stick around here until Benoit comes out. I've told Costello that if he spills the beans we'll close him up and give him the fare-thee-well."

"I'm going to make a report to my boss. I may see you later."

Lethbridge nodded, and, lighting a fresh cigarette, idled along Greek Street, taking good care to keep the entrance to the other street well in view.

Cramer walked swiftly into Old Compton Street, and found a taxi. Telling the man to drive to Regent Street, he climbed in and sank back, he was carrying a grouch, for his old friend's words had worried him, made him uneasy and suspicious as well. More than that the old sore had been opened up. It had galled him to find Lethbridge trailing the same quarry under such different auspices. He hadn't been quite frank with Lethbridge out of pride. In his heart of hearts he had already felt more than one twinge of suspicion of Markheim, but he had smothered the feeling as soon as it lifted its head, for Markheim was paying him good money, and Cramer needed it.

Nevertheless, the old training would assert itself, and he had to confess to himself that it was queer that a French jewel crook should make tracks for Markheim's offices as soon as he landed in London. If Scotland Yard was on the job and some backwash might catch Markheim it might be wise for him to stand out from under as Lethbridge had suggested.

He was just in time to catch Markheim, who was on the point of leaving. Had Cramer arrived after his employer's departure he would, in the ordinary way, give a guarded report to the clerk who had Markheim's private telephone number, and would pass it along in that way.

Markheim gave a sharp glance at his private sleuth. He saw plainly enough that something had arisen to perturb Cramer.

"Well?"

Cramer made his report briefly but concisely. When he finished Markheim sat down at his desk and tapped the mahogany thoughtfully.

"So he went to a punk hotel in Soho and saw a man of the name of Acier?"

"Yes, sir."

"This is important if Acier is the person I think he must be. Are you sure there is no room for mistake?"

"None, sir. And I think I'd better tell you that we are not the only people who are interested in Benoit's movements."

Markheim shot him a swift look, and frowned.

"Benoit —how did you know that was his name? I didn't tell you."

"No, sir; I learned it after leaving here."

"You have been thorough." There was a faint sneer in Markheim's voice that brought a flush of anger to Cramer's face, but he offered no retort. Then: "You say other people are interested in Benoit —who are they?"

"I am sorry that I am not at liberty to tell you, sir."

"What the devil do you mean? You are working for me, aren't you?"

"I was told in confidence. But I can give you some more information, sir. This man Benoit is a well-known French crook."

"You have said too much or too little. I pay you your money, and yet you say you cannot tell me what other people are interested in Benoit. Is it the police?"

"I am not at liberty to disclose my source of information, sir."

"But I insist on knowing. You'll give me a full report, or you finish here and now."

"Very well, sir."

"You refuse?"

"I cannot tell you."

"You are a fool. It is plain enough now why you were kicked out of Scotland Yard. You didn't think I knew that, did you? But I don't take on any man until I know all about him, and I learned what was necessary about you. Once more —do you tell me?"

"No."

Markheim leaned over and pressed the button. When the door opened to admit the clerk, he rapped:

"Pay this man what is coming to him and see him off the premises!"

Then he shot a look of cold anger at Cramer. "Get out!" he snarled.

And Cramer went.

Markheim would have been better advised to have used the velvet glove instead of the bludgeon.

Chapter 13. Markheim's Victims.

FOR twenty years Junius Markheim had devoted all his facilities to one end —financial independence.

His activities had never been exercised before in England. As a young man, adopting the confidence game as his profession, he had determined to keep England as the one place to which he could retire when the time came. But almost every other part of the globe had seen his gross figure at some time or other.

An iron nerve, brains, and the knowledge how to use them, a supreme self-confidence and a more than ordinary capacity for detail had stood him in good stead. He had done consistently well, but never, until he stumbled on the knowledge of the De Santos treasure, had he come across the big thing for which he had been seeking.

And, up to the day when Romer Walmsley had turned up on the scene, he had felt no misgivings. He had always expected Walmsley to show up one day, and he had been ready. Let him dispose of the treasure in one lump, and he would call "Finis." It wouldn't be difficult to take care of Walmsley. If he wouldn't listen to reason he must be put where he couldn't cause further mischief.

Not for one moment had Markheim felt a twinge of uneasiness — not until Cramer made his report about Benoit and Acier.

But now a nasty suspicion began to form in Markheim's mind. If Benoit was indeed a crook, as Cramer said, then what was his game about the emeralds? Did he have any suspicion that whatever title Markheim gave to them might be open to question?

Was Acier a crook as well, and not the respectable jewel broker he had held himself out to be? Was he —Junius Markheim —being led up the garden after all these years? And who were the other people who were interested in Benoit? If it was the police, then he — Markheim —must bring things to a head quickly. Cramer might be wrong; he would know the truth by that night. And if Benoit were genuine, then he would finish off the business just the same.

His thoughts did not improve his temper as he drove back into Sussex. Markheim laid his plans so carefully that a check such as Cramer's report made him suspicious of everything and everybody. Hence he was in an unpleasant frame of mind when he reached his house and learned of the strenuous doings there during his absence.

He listened to Jose's report before entering the house. The man made a plain statement of the escape of Walmsley and the chase. He indicated that the wounded had been taken to the loft over the stable, which had been turned into a dormitory for the guards, and their wounds treated there.

He had deemed it unwise to send for any doctor in the district, as he had sufficient knowledge of such wounds to treat them.

"But how did he get away?" demanded Markheim. "He was in your charge. How did he get rid of his bonds?"

"Senor, I cannot answer. He was seen to burst forth from the house and run. I have since been to the place where he was a prisoner. I found —this."

As he spoke, he turned and, pushing aside some sacks, held up the severed bits of rope which had bound Walmsley. Markheim's eyes narrowed to mere slits as he examined them. He didn't need any more to tell him that treachery within his own house was being flaunted before him.

"I'll attend to this!" he snarled. "Get your men patched up. I may make a quick move. And who can't come will have to shift for themselves. You've got the closed van —see that it is in order. And I want the big saloon got ready at once."

He strode swiftly to the front porch and passed through the hall. Half-way down he threw open the door of the long sitting-room, where Carlotta was sitting in a low chair, with some bits of embroidery on her shoulder was the macaw.

She sent a swift glance at Markheim and, despite her efforts at self-control, a deep blush rose in her cheeks. Markheim's eyes bored through and through her.

"Well," came the snarling question through his thick lips, "just what part did you play in Walmsley's get-away?"

Her voice showed more control than her features.

"I knew you would accuse me when you returned. I know nothing about it."

"Then who cut his bonds? Don't lie to me! I've seen them, and someone inside this house has double-crossed me. If it wasn't you, who was it?"

She shrugged, but gave no answer. Markheim uttered an oath and strode towards her. His great hands went out as if he would take her throat and squeeze the truth out of her. But as he bent forward she flashed a pearl-handled revolver from beneath the embroidery material.

"If you touch me, Junius, I'll kill you!" she said tensely. "I have told you the truth. I knew nothing about the escape until I heard the shooting. Leave me alone. You can't afford to quarrel with me."

"Then who was it? There is only one other person, for it wasn't the girl."

"I have no more to say. You would do better to tell me how things went in London. You haven't heard the last of Walmsley. He will come again and when he does, he won't be alone. I tell you, I would have killed him if I had known he was escaping."

Markheim slammed the door and mounted the stairs to the top floor. Passing down the hall to the suite occupied by Julia de Santos, he tapped at the door and entered. He gave only a brief nod to the girl, who was sitting in her chair reading, then he beckoned to the woman in black. She rose and followed him into the hall. He closed the door and walked along a few yards. Then he turned suddenly, thrusting his big face close to hers.

"What have you got to say about Walmsley?"

"Nothing."

"Did you cut him loose?"

She made no reply. Markheim grasped her wrist and twisted it until it must have given her agony, but she did not flinch.

"I should have put you away years ago," he said thickly. "Someone in this house has double-crossed me to-day. Carlotta says she knows nothing about it. There is only you. You think you are going to get away with this obstinate silence. Listen to me, you she-devil! I've stood all from you that I'm going to stand. This thing comes to a head to-day. Then I'm finished. If you want to save your bacon, you get that girl in a frame of mind to sign—by tonight. After that I'll see that you have no further chance for mischief. I was a fool to let you in at all."

Her strange eyes held him in a steady gaze.

"I'll do just as it suits me," she said quietly. "If I had had any fear of you, Junius Markheim, I should have shown it years ago. I know you as no one else knows you. And your threats do not frighten me. The reckoning can come to-night as well as another time, I am ready. Now let me go."

He was panting heavily, and for a moment it looked as if he would strike the woman down where she stood. But something in the cold stare of her eyes thwarted his will. He threw her back against the wall, with a string of curses that were appalling in their vehemence. But his words left her unmoved. Again, as on many other occasions, her will had proved the stronger —too tenacious for him to break the chains which linked them together.

But she was right; those chains were to be snapped that night, yet not as Junius Markheim planned.

At four o'clock Markheim telephoned through to the Hotel Venetia and got hold of Benoit. During the time that had elapsed since Cramer made his report, he had given a good deal of thought to what the latter's words had roused in his mind. He was suspicious of Benoit, yet, beyond what he had been told about Acier's presence in London, and the type of hotel where Benoit had met him, he had nothing of a definitely suspicious nature to go on.

On the other hand, it was curious that Benoit should have stated so definitely in his office that Acier was in Paris and that he would get him on the trunk line during the day. Until Cramer put the suspicion into his mind he had entertained not the slightest doubt of Benoit. Nor could he bring himself to believe now that the man was not all right.

For three years Markheim had worked with patient method to brings about a disposal of the De Santos treasure, most of which was in the form of uncut emeralds collected by the Spanish conquistadores of old. He knew that it would be a matter of utmost delicacy to do so. If such a quantity were to appear in one lot, questions were bound to be asked. He had watched each step carefully and had assured himself that Acier, the Paris jewel broker, was a thoroughly dependable man. What he did not know was that the "Acier" who had come to London was an impostor, a former clerk of the jewel broker's, who had full knowledge of Markheim's tentative proposals to his employer and had brought away with him copies of that correspondence. In Benoit he had found the shrewd brain he needed to formulate as pretty a plot as could be devised. Between them they had suborned a fellow-clerk in Acier's employ, had had business letter-paper printed exactly similar to that used by the jewel broker and, through the agency of the other clerk, had succeeded in getting hold of every letter that Markheim wrote on the subject. In other words, an active correspondence had been carried on in Acier's name, of which he knew absolutely nothing; nor, until Cramer had stated that Benoit was a notorious jewel crook, did Junius Markheim suspect for a moment that all was not as it should be.

•   •   •   •   •

At the very moment when Junius Markheim was on the line to Benoit, ex-Detective-sergeant Cramer was running the gauntlet of his old colleagues at Scotland Yard, on his way to Inspector Lethbridge. As he was shown into the small, unattractive room, Lethbridge gave him a quick, scrutinising glance.

"Well, George, going to take my advice?"

"I'm going to be honest with you. I've parted company with Markheim —never mind why. I'd like a chance to go after Benoit, if you will let me in on it. I can tell you where Markheim lives, if that is worth anything to you. I want a chance to come back."

"You'll get it if I can manage it, George. Sit over there and say nothing. There is someone else waiting, and I want to hear what he has to spill this time. Maybe you'll be interested."

Once more the door opened, and this time Sexton Blake and Romer Walmsley were shown in by a constable.

Chapter 14.   Benoit Shows His Hand.

AT precisely ten o'clock that evening a large, black limousine drew into the kerb at the corner of Chester Street and Belgrave Square.

Even had the evening been fine there would have been few pedestrians passing that quiet spot at the hour, and on this night only an occasional motor was to be seen, for heavy masses of banked clouds and vivid flashes of lightning to the east told of a severe electrical storm approaching from Essex and Kent.

It was the culmination of a hot day, and since the mounting storm had brought dusk earlier than usual, it well suited the purpose of the big man in dark blue chauffeur's uniform who sat at the wheel of the waiting limousine.

In approaching the kerb, he had brought the car round so it faced in the direction of Grosvenor Place, and parallel to the blank side-wall of a big corner residence. From this position he could see anyone coming on foot from Grosvenor Place; and, indeed, he had been waiting for less than ten minutes, when two figures swung into view. At the same moment a taxi crossed the other end of Chester Street — obviously the cab from which they had stepped

They came along at a brisk walk until they were almost opposite the big car. Here the taller of the two paused and peered at the bulky figure on the box.

"You have come from?" he asked in a low tone.

"Mr. 'X.'"

Without further words the two pedestrians entered and sank back against the luxurious cushions. Immediately, the car started, the driver swinging round the end of Belgrave Square into Eaton Place, and thence through Sloane Square to pick up the King's Road.

The two passengers either had nothing to say to each other, or had agreed that no words should be exchanged on the journey, for, from the moment they took their places, neither uttered a sound — until, when the limousine was just passing Chelsea Town Hall, a slight, clattering noise drew from the taller a suppressed exclamation.

In one swift moment the lights of King's Road had been completely cut off, leaving them in darkness. This lasted for but a moment, the interior of the car becoming brightly illuminated by a bulb that nestled in the upholstery at the top.

The taller of the two reached out his fingers and touched a shiny black substance that now shuttered the nearest window. His companion imitated his example; then they looked at each other significantly. They had no need to explore farther. The car was now effectively sealed from the gaze of anyone outside, and the two inside could see nothing of the route they were following.

They accepted the situation philosophically. In a rack at one side was a silver box containing cigars, and beside it a flask of whisky with, in a lower rack, a diminutive siphon of soda. Benoit —for the taller of the two was he —found two glasses, and poured drinks. His companion, a wiry little man dressed in typical French fashion, and outwardly sufficiently like Jules Acier, the famous French gem dealer, to have caused that individual to rub his own eyes in astonishment, accepted the drink with a smile and a nod, but still made no remark. Those two knew the value of caution in their profession, and they knew, likewise, the detective possibilities of a microphone.

The limousine seemed to them gradually to increase its speed, until they were travelling along at a high rate. Having little knowledge of England outside London the precaution of the automatic shutters was hardly necessary, for they would have found it difficult, even if they could see, to guess whither they were bound; but with the blank windows as an impenetrable obstacle they were completely at sea. But that did not worry the two jewel crooks, for they felt perfectly capable of turning the cards to their own advantage when the right moment should arrive.

From time to time, as they sped along, a noise as of booming artillery penetrated to the interior of the car. At first the intervals were infrequent, but as time passed they shortened steadily until an almost continuous uproar of swelling, thunderous clamour was beating about them.

They were conscious, too, of a rocking motion which was by no possible chance due to the vibration of the powerful engine, which purred with such obvious reserve of power; nor could it be put down to roughness of the road, for the bumping which would have been a necessary concomitant was absent.

The thunderous racket and the swaying motion reached a pitch at last that caused the two passengers to regard each other anxiously; but still the vehicle forged on its way, while the hands of the clock that was set in an ivory frame at one side showed midnight.

Five minutes, ten minutes, a quarter of an hour more went by, and then the car slowed down gradually, seemed to swing sharply, and came to a stop. At almost the same instant the shutters which had closed so mysteriously flew back, the overhead bulb went out, and the pair found themselves looking upon a lighted porch.

Their vision was obscured for a moment as a bulky figure stepped close and opened the door. The outer livery that had disguised him so well had been thrown aside, and now they saw that it was none other than Markheim himself who had acted as chauffeur.

He nodded his great head carelessly.

"I thought you would guess, gentlemen. It was wiser that I should go to meet you. Enter, please, for the storm is getting even more violent.

They stepped out quickly just as a vivid flash of lightning lit up their surroundings, playing about the house as if it must seek contact at some point. The resultant crash came so close on its heels as to sound as a splitting rattle rather than a booming roar and, to the accompaniment of this, the crooks dashed through the porch.

Markheim threw open the front door and ushered them into the hall. Down this he led the way and into the study, where now there was no sign of the thick glass partition that had befooled Walmsley.

Markheim had prepared his stage carefully for this meeting. He was making the mistake of giving little weight to what Cramer had told him. On the other hand, he felt himself perfectly capable of dealing with his visitors if there should be any truth in the report that Benoit was an International jewel crook. At the same time, Junius Markheim could not believe he could have been deceived so completely.

For nearly three years now —ever since he had got things ready for launching his great treasure into a private market —he had taken each step with extreme care. It is true that he had not personally visited Paris in order to make contact with Acier on his own ground, but every confidential report he had had on the man was of the most satisfactory nature. Then how could there be anything wrong, he asked himself.

Benoit was acting for Acier. His correspondence direct to Acier had been acknowledged promptly and his replies received on Acier's own business paper. Hatton Garden knew the broker well; the name was one that brought immediate recognition wherever it was mentioned among circles of gem dealers.

And even in the different quarters where Markheim had cautiously disposed of a few emeralds now and then in order to secure ready funds for carrying on, he had heard it said that the finer stones would eventually find their way to Acier, of Paris. Cramer had got hold of some fool idea, he told himself, or else had been trying to double-cross him. Just as well the fellow had been sacked.

Yet he was cautious, and for that reason had made his preparations before driving to town to pick up his two guests. There was nothing of suspicious nature in the way he drew forward two easy chairs close to the big desk, where he took his own seat.

Nor was there any sign in that luxuriously furnished room that Markheim had half a dozen different traps which he could spring by the mere touch of a button within a foot of his hand. It was all regular and perfectly open in appearance. He did not know that other forces had been active that same evening, nor that he and his guests were not the only shadows that had come out of the storm.

Markheim had refreshments ready at hand and when three glasses had been charged with whisky and soda he looked first at Benoit, then at "Acier," seeing the latter for the first time as a foppish little man, typically French and with deep-set, jumpy, dark eyes that indicated high nervous tension.

"Well, gentlemen," he said suavely, "we have arrived and there is no need of losing time. I am prepared to carry out my part of the arrangement when you have shown me the guarantee mentioned."

Both men bowed slightly, and Benoit motioned towards his companion.

"You mean the amount we are prepared to pay as a deposit —but certainly, monsieur, Monsieur Acier will produce it."

The smaller man drew out a long, blue envelope from the inside pocket of his coat and extracted a slip of paper. He passed this to Markheim, who, scrutinising it, found it to be a sight draft on Messrs. Lazard Freres, the rich and important private banking firm of Paris, whose ramifications are world-wide. It looked like a perfectly good piece of paper to Markheim, and he could scarcely be called careless in accepting it as genuine, considering it was the work of the most expert forger in Europe.

He pushed it away, though his fingers itched to retain it. His eyes were sparkling with a new light as he looked up.

"And the balance?" he asked softly.

"Acier" smiled and took out another slip of paper. It needed all Markheim's self-control to keep his hands from trembling as he examined this second document and saw that it was a sight draft on the same banking firm for nine hundred thousand pounds.

"I came prepared, monsieur," remarked "Acier" with a slight lisp that would have been recognised quickly enough at the Paris Surete. "It is as Monsieur Benoit told you over the telephone this afternoon —the business is of such importance that I thought it better to lend my eyes to an examination of the stones. Voila! There is now no reason for delay if you are satisfied,"

"I'm satisfied all right," muttered Markheim.

And yet he hesitated. Now that everything was going so smoothly he felt a sudden uneasiness. Yet he could see no flaw. He was on his own ground, inside his own stronghold. True, Walmsley had got away, and that indicated treachery among his own people, but Walmsley could hardly show up again before another day, even if he had the nerve. And since Walmsley was only after a share of the treasure, he wouldn't dare go to the police for aid.

The only thing yet to complete was the signing of the document by Julia de Santos and that should be ready by now. Carlotta had had her orders and had promised to get it from the girl by some means before his return from town. She should have it now. She would be waiting for the signal. He would give it to her.

Pushing his hand forward a little, he pressed one of the buttons on the battery on the desk; then he rose.

"Very well, gentlemen, I am satisfied, and I think you will not regret your journey. I shall show you the largest and finest collection of jewels in Europe, in the world. There are diamonds and rubies and sapphires, as I told you, but the bulk of the collection consists of emeralds such as not even you, Monsieur Acier, have ever gazed upon. Just a few moments."

With that Markheim turned to the wall at the back of the desk and pressed a part of the wood paneling. As the pressure released a secret spring, a whole section of the oak slid aside, to reveal a big steel door measuring about five feet high by three feet wide. Set in the armour plain was a nickelled combination which Markheim began to turn, keeping his back so that his two guests could not possibly see at what points on the disc the indicator paused.

When he had made a series of four turns and reverses he took hold of a nickelled handle and pressed it back, drawing towards him as he did so. The big door swung outwards without a sound, revealing an inner door of sheet steel which Markheim unlocked with a key.

The interior was shadowy, but when he reached inside and pressed a switch, the whole place was illuminated by a brilliant light that was thrown back in sharp reflection from the glass surfaces of a row of what looked like show-cases on a shelf about waist high.

Markheim took one look at the cases, assuring himself that the contents were all in order; then he drew back into the room and signed to his two guests to enter.

All three found it difficult to remain perfectly calm in that moment, but their suppressed agitation was far from being due to the same cause.

"Acier" led the way round the desk and inclined his head slightly as Markheim bade him step inside the strong-room; Benoit followed and took up a place beside "Acier" just as the latter threw up his hands with an exclamation of amazement at the glittering sight.

Markheim moved in close behind them and thus the position for the briefest moment covered by "Acier's" ejaculation. On the next instant Markheim saw both men in front perform a right-about that could only have been achieved by practice, and then, from nowhere, it seemed, flashed two automatic pistols to back up the threat of two pairs of eyes that were glittering with the intent of the killer.

In one vivid flash understanding came to Junius Markheim. The whole fabric, as it were, became unrolled before the searchlight of his mind. He had blundered in a major sense, but not irrevocably, for his own safety.

He knew in that moment that Cramer had told the truth. Benoit and "Acier" were crooks. But they were likewise fools to think they could catch Junius Markheim napping so easily. Gone in that same flash was all his careful work of three years. He knew it. He had walked on to a quicksand, but he still clutched safety.

With an agility amazing in one of his bulk, he sprang backwards to the door of the strong-room. Benoit and "Acier" leaped after him, but Markheim's hand was already feeling for a button set just beneath the light switch, and then, as he pressed it, he backed quickly on to the steel threshold against which his heels had already clicked.

The result of that one touch was appallingly sudden. One moment the two crooks were clawing at him, each using a hand, while two guns were beginning to spit a hail of lead; the next the whole floor of the strong-room was dropping swiftly from its level, causing the startled crooks to spin about like a pair of marionettes.

Bullets whistled past Markheim's ears, bullets thudded into the steel walls of the strong-room, bullets shattered the thick plateglass of the showcases, but not one struck the big man who was now laughing at the antics of his victims.

In one desperate effort to recover Benoit leaped towards the door. His weapon fell, his fingers gripped the ridge of the steel frame, he drew himself up until his face was above the level, his eyes narrowed in his determination to reach Markheim, and haul him down if he could not drag himself up.

Markheim waited until his chin was just over the edge, then, with another laugh, he drew back his booted foot and smashed it with terrific force full into Benoit's face. The crook gave a shriek of agony, his fingers slid from their grasp, and he dropped a dozen feet to the bottom of the pit that had been made by the descending floor.

Once more Markheim laughed, then he drew back, closed the inner panel of sheet steel, locked it, slammed the heavy armour-plate door, and gave the combination a twirl.

He turned back to the desk, and was reaching for a button that would summon Jose, when there came a hammering at the door of the study, and, without waiting for Markheim's permission, Jose burst into the room.

His face was smeared with blood, and he was panting as if he had run a long distance.

"Senor —master!" he gasped.

Markheim sprang towards him, but before he covered half the distance he was brought to a stop by a dreadful tumult that seemed to come from the upper part of the house.

Chapter 15.   The End of the House of Silence.

A TERRIFIC crash of thunder drowned the medley of screams that had caused the tumult.

But Markheim paid little attention to the angry explosion of the elements. His ears had been hammered with so many assaults of a like nature all the way from London that they had ceased to flinch under the blows.

It was the other sounds of a different timbre that had caused him to freeze in his tracks, for, out of the confused uproar, he had been able to identify two contributory voices —one was Carlotta's, pitched high in hysterical abandon; the other was the wanton screech of the macaw.

With the dying away of the thunder in reluctant, complaining rumbles, the racket broke out afresh, but again it was submerged by a fresh invasion of shattering sound.

Standing in the middle of the study, Markheim could see along the wide hall past the black oak staircase to the front door. And now, at this fresh outbreak, he saw the heavy portal crash inwards and a body of men stream in across the wreckage.

He recognised ex-Detective-sergeant Cramer in the van, and then his quick, searching eyes fixed on other figures that only one description fitted —police.

He shot out one huge hand and hauled Jose clear of the door just as the whole body of men rushed down the hall.

But by the time they were opposite the staircase the heavy study door slammed, and, inside the room, Junius Markheim pressed one of the many buttons that he had had fitted to this sinister house that caused a steel shutter to rise swiftly from the floor and fill the whole aperture of the door.

"Quick, Jose!" he gasped. "Here, to the centre of the room. Turn round —so. Be ready for the drop, and then slide. I'll follow."

The mestizo obeyed quickly. He had already practised that drop, in case of just such an emergency as this. His fashion of going down would not land him at the bottom as Walmsley had struck, for he knew the trick of the thing.

Markheim was already close to the wall near the safe. There were two buttons controlling the trap in the floor, one on a table at the other end of the room, which he had touched on the occasion of Walmsley's first visit; the other among the small battery of those close to the safe. He pressed the latter. At once the section of floor dropped from sight, Jose disappearing in a slide as it did so.

Markheim paused to listen to the terrific assault on the door, smiled as he snapped his fingers in defiance, then, for all his bulk, disappeared through the trap as easily as had Jose. A few moments later the floor section snapped back into place.

Out in the hall, the crowd from Scotland Yard, Walmsley, Sexton Blake, and the local police from Horsham were still driving human wedges against the heavy oak, which, though it strained more and more under the repented assaults, was still unyielding owing to the steel panel that now backed it.

Beneath, in the secret chamber where Walmsley had lain confined, all was brilliantly lighted. At one end of the long, low, narrow chamber was a steel door, at which Markheim was working with a key. Close at hand stood Jose, an automatic pistol trained on the edge of the door.

Markheim's sudden jump back was his signal. In the same moment the door swung open, and out of the safe behind staggered Benoit and "Acier." Confused by what had happened, they were unprepared for the swiftness of Jose's attack. He shot once, twice, and at each report a man lurched forward on his face.

Markheim gave a grunt of approval, and leaped over the two prostrate bodies into the interior of the safe. Grasping a strong leather bag that lay on the floor, he reversed his own weapon, and smashed what remained of the glass in the cases where the precious gems still glittered.

Sweep after sweep his hand went until the whole mass had been tumbled into the bag. He snapped it shut as he jumped back across the two dead men, and, without waiting for orders, Jose dragged them inside again.

Markheim slammed the steel door, locked it, and followed Jose, who was already racing towards the opposite wall The mestizo knew the trick of a secret panel there as well as Markheim, for he had used it often enough. It was not the door by which Walmsley had been admitted to the open grounds, but opened into a narrow tunnel that swallowed Markheim's bulk in a flash as he plunged through.

Jose followed. The secret panel was closed, and now Markheim pressed a switch that served two purposes; it turned on the lights in the tunnel, while, at the same moment, it switched off those in the secret chamber they had just left.

On the left of the passage was a grill, inside which a bulb lit up what looked like the interior of a small, automatic lift. Markheim passed the leather bag to Jose while he dragged back the grill. He stepped into the lift and jerked a hand at Jose.

"Keep both ways covered, and shoot at once if anyone gets through. I shall be back in a few minutes. Be ready to go on."

"Si, senor."

Just what methods Junius Markheim had used to inspire such loyally in the mestizo, Jose, may not be known. But in him he had a far worthier servant than he deserved, and one whose devotion would have served him well to a better purpose.

When Markheim pressed a control button inside, the lift shot up out of sight, passing the lower floors of the house until it came to rest on the top floor. Here Markheim stepped into a small closet, which, in turn, admitted him to the bedroom adjoining the sitting-room where he kept Julia de Santos prisoner.

On the moment of his appearance he surprised a strange tableau. Seated in her long chair, languid, yet still resisting, was Julia, while over her stood Carlotta in a state of hysterical rage at the girl's steady refusal to sign the piece of paper which Carlotta was waving in her face. It was evident to Markheim that neither Carlotta nor Julia knew yet of the invasion of the police, but it was obvious enough that the crisis had not missed the gaunt woman in black who stood on the threshold, her attention divided between the racket below and the rage of Carlotta.

To add to the confused din, the macaw, realising that its mistress was in a rage, was screaming shrilly, while it swooped back and forth close to Julia's head, its flapping wings almost striking her in each passage, and its deadly beak snapping viciously within an inch of her white neck.

Markheim's eyes shot stark venom at the woman in black. But that was the only attention he gave her. Rushing forward, he pushed Carlotta aside while he bent down and swooped the girl, Julia, into his great arms.

"Into the lift!" he snapped. "Police —no time to lose —"

Carlotta broke off her hysterical fit and stared at him. The big crook did not wait to see if he was obeyed. He was already making for the bed-room with his burden, while Julia struggled feebly against that overpowering hold.

Then, suddenly, Carlotta seemed to realise what he meant. She snapped her fingers at the macaw, bringing it to rest on her shoulder; then she followed Markheim.

Scarcely had they passed into the bedroom than the room they had just left seemed to split asunder with a terrific flash of brilliancy. An appalling crash followed, and then the air became filled with a sulphurous smell that told its own tale. Lightning had struck very close.

The woman in black had fallen back into the hall as the blinding shaft of lightning struck, but, though half-blinded and with one hand wiping across her eyes feebly, she endeavoured to get across the room and catch up the others.

A burst of flame drove her back, and as she staggered again into the hall she felt herself gripped by a pair of strong arms that picked her up and carried her along to the head of the stairs.

As for Markheim, he was already in the lift, his burden on the floor and Carlotta crowding close to him. He did not wait for the woman in black. The sight of the flames already bursting through the open doorway caused his eyes to glitter at the thought of what might have occurred.

"I hope it gets her!" he snarled as he slammed the door and pressed the button. "Keep your eye on the girl," he added to Carlotta. "We've got a chance yet. Let them hammer their cursed arms off."

They struck the bottom with a distinct thud. Jose was waiting as he had been left, and as soon as Markheim was out and had Julia in his arms, he started along the tunnel, Carlotta and the macaw bringing up the rear.

The passage wound after the fashion of a great letter "S," covering a matter of some two hundred full paces. Junius Markheim had not built it in its entirety, but he had lengthened and adapted an old tunnel that had existed there for a long time and the existence of which had been one of the chief things to influence him in taking that old place in Sussex and installing other fittings that would serve him in just such an emergency as this.

At the end was another door, barred on the inner side. Jose flipped up the bar and stepped straight into a cellar, stone-floored, stone-walled, and with heavy oaken planks for a ceiling. It was, in fact, directly beneath the ground floor of the larger stable, though there was only one outward thing to betray that it might exist. That was a pair of double wide doors at the rear of the stable, which were quite invisible from the front of the building.

Here, as in the passage, electric light had been provided on a lavish scale. The same system of two-way switches prevailed, that which shut off the current in the passage turning on the illumination in the cellar.

When Jose had pressed the switch there was revealed but one item to proclaim the use of the place.

This was a big, black, closed motor-van standing with its radiator pointing towards the double doors. It was Junius Markheim's "emergency" vehicle —the same which he had warned Jose to have ready for the use of the wounded men who still lay in the loft. Had he not been so pressed for time he would have made personal use of the large limousine that had brought Benoit and "Acier" from London; but with the police dogs growling at his heels his own safety must come first —that and the possession of Julia de Santos and the jewels.

Carlotta was a secondary consideration. She could come or remain. Jose counted as himself. The woman in black was, he hoped, already nothing but a mass of charred bones. The others must shift for themselves. For Junius Markheim had not overlooked the possibility of being pressed as hard or even harder. There was another haven that would shelter him —if he could reach it. And he had by no means sprung his last box of tricks on his pursuers.

It took very few moments to bundle Julia de Santos and the bag of jewels into the van with Carlotta and the macaw to keep guard. Jose was closing the doors, which locked automatically, while Markheim was already clambering into the seat.

Jose flung himself in after as the self-starter sent the engine off with a steady thrum. There was no need to open the doors. As the front wheels passed over a metal plate in the floor the two leaves swung open, admitting the passage of the car, and then, as the black wheels cleared, they closed with a soft thud.

Junius Markheim brought the van round into the main gravelled drive. The worst of the gauntlet was yet to be run, for, in order to reach the outer road leading up the valley, he must pass the front porch of the house. But by the time he was almost opposite that the van was leaping into full speed, appearing like a sinister vision as it rushed out of the penumbra of light from the open hall door.

Yet it did not get past without its mission being read by two watchers, and, while it was still visible in that path of radiance, one form might have been seen to spring down the steps and make a violent spring towards the man at the wheel.

While Markheim was coolly carrying out plans he had rehearsed many a time, the police gang in the hall had been pounding the door of the library to pieces. When the sheet of steel became visible, Sexton Blake drew back and caught Walmsley's arm.

"Is this the only way in? This fellow is going to give us the slip if we don't watch out."

"We can reach another door through the music-room."

"Then let's try it. Come on, Lethbridge, and you, Cramer. Leave the others at this one!"

Walmsley led the way into the music-room which he had penetrated on his first disastrous visit. At the end was the door he had spoken of, and this gave no resistance as they lurched against it. They poured over the threshold, Blake finding a switch to reveal the long stretch of the library, undisturbed, untenanted.

Before Walmsley remembered about the heavy glass panel that had separated him from Markheim, Blake, Lethbridge and Cramer were rushing down the room to bring up with a crash against the invisible barrier. Walmsley called out a warning too late; explained matters in a breath, and pointed to the spot in the floor where the trap now lay flush.

"That is the place I told you about," he jerked to Blake. "I forgot to warn you about the glass. We can't get through here —it is too thick. Anyway —no use. Markheim will be making for the grounds. We'd better try and cut him off there."

Blake waited for no more. He was wondering what could have become of Benoit and "Acier," but, in comparison with the importance of catching Markheim, they could wait.

It was Blake who led the race back through the music-room to the hall. The rest of the police had desisted from assaulting the other door, and the inspector from Horsham was running up the stairs followed by two constables, while the rest remained grouped at the bottom.

Everyone had been conscious of the furious crash that had followed the terrific flush of lightning a few moments before, but in the determination to lay hands on Markheim had paid little attention to it.

But now, smoke was already coming down from the upper floors, driven by some strong draught that was finding its way in on that level. Realising that whoever was above might be trapped by the sudden out break of fire, Blake and Walmsley swarmed up after the other three.

They reached the first floor in a swirl of smoke and made a rapid circuit of the rooms there, finding them empty. They raced up the second flight just in time to meet the Horsham inspector at the top with a woman in his arms. They attempted again and again to fight through the smoke and flames towards the seat of the fire, but were driven back, and then, as they retreated to the first floor, Walmsley caught Blake's arm.

"No use here. He'll reach the grounds in the way I escaped."

Blake did not answer, but, turning, sped back to the ground floor and out on to the porch; Walmsley was close on his heels. They arrived there just in time to see a black shape lurch out of the gloom and pass through the path of light that streamed from the hall door. They needed no more than that fleeting vision to guess what had happened, and while the black van was still revealed by the light Blake took a flying leap that carried him clean on to the gravelled drive.

A second spring enabled him to get his fingers on the arm of the seat. He was flung along several yards, but managed to get his feet on to the step. The man at the wheel, whom he could see well enough now and recognised as the man he had glimpsed for a moment in the library, paid him no attention —just bent low, watching the way ahead while the powerful engine rose higher and higher to a maximum output of energy.

But, crouching beside him was Jose, his savage little eyes glittering in the backwash of the reflection. With a wary eye on him, Blake threw up his free hand and jammed his automatic into Markheim's ribs. The act was the touch of a fuse to Jose. With a low, inarticulate cry he reached over the big man's hunched shoulders and thrust down at Blake with a knife.

"Stop, Markheim —stop!"

Blake was roaring the command even as the point of the knife plunged between his fingers and ripped into the padded leather of the seat arm. Jose dragged the knife clear and raised it again, but before he could make a second downthrust Markheim lurched heavily to one side, jerking his massive shoulders as he did so. The weight caught Blake just under the chin, his body was swung backwards, his pistol barked harmlessly in the air as he dragged on the trigger. He made a desperate effort to recover, but Markheim swung the car sharply to the left, the lurch pitching Blake heavily to the gravelled drive, where he hit on his shoulder and rolled over and over with the terrific impetus the speed of the car had given him.

He was vaguely conscious that big iron gates loomed just ahead. He came to a stop in a half-sitting posture, almost stunned from the force of his fall. Yet he strove to discern what Markheim was up to as he kept the big van close to the edge of the gravel yet at the same terrific speed that seemed too much to throttle down and brake to a stop before he hit the iron barricade.

But then Blake saw a thing that brought his wandering senses back to normal with a jerk. He saw the huge gates swing open widely, swiftly as if the invisible hands of a giant had thrust them back. He saw the van leap through the opening and plunge down the sloping road to the stone bridge; and then he saw the gates, now but dimly outlined, crash back into place. It was only some time later that he ferreted out the mystery when he discovered a cunningly concealed metal control plate set in the ground at one side of the drive that operated the gates by electrical contact just as the plate in the cellar under the stable controlled the doors there.

He was conscious that Walmsley was bending over him.

"Are you all right, Mr. Blake?"

"I think so," growled Blake, as he got stiffly to his feet, realising as his hands mechanically felt his limbs that one side of his coat was ripped to shreds, and that a myriad of small gravel grains were pitted in his skin. "Did you see that car go through the gates, Walmsley, or did I only imagine it?"

"It went through all right, but I don't know how the gates opened and shut. I was trying to haul myself up at the back. I heard shots; I wondered if they had got you. Then I saw you rolling clear."

"The shots were mine, but missed. We'd better find out what has happened back at the house. Markheim was driving the car and he has got clear. We'd better tell Lethbridge and Cramer."

As they retraced their way up the drive they met the two men from Scotland Yard racing towards them.

"What was it?" jerked Lethbridge.

Blake explained.

"You'd better warn the Horsham inspector, Lethbridge. He may make for the coast, or he may make for London. Still again he may have another bolthole. I'm beginning to acquire a very deep respect for that crook. What have you found at the house?"

"Nothing much. Wait until we get round this turn of the drive and you will, see why."

For some moments now Blake had been conscious of a red glow ahead, but it was not until they got past the next bend in the drive that he realised it came from the whole area of the mansion. The roof seemed ablaze from end to end, and most of the windows of the top and first floor showed greedy flames licking through them. That the place was doomed was evident, and as he realised that other human beings should be inside those walls Blake drew up.

"Markheim and the dago, who ran down the hall as we entered the house, were in the front seat of the van," he said hurriedly. "There may have been others inside the van, Lethbridge; I don't know. But how many have you got out? What about the two French crooks?"

"Heaven alone knows, Blake. We've got one person only —a very queer sort of middle-aged woman who won't say a word. We were driven back by the flames. I don't know what to say about the two French crooks. I wanted to talk to you. But we have found a nice collection of specimens in one of the lofts over the stable. Most of them are wounded, so I take it Mr. Walmsley can tell us about them."

"Part of Markheim's gang," agreed Walmsley. "I'll soon identify them. I'd like to have a look at the woman you rescued."

They were almost as close to the house by now as the flames would permit them to go. The inspector from Horsham and the constables had rounded up the men found in the loft, keeping them standing by in the stable for the time being. One of the constables had been sent off to put through a fire call, though it was plain that nothing could be done now to save the mansion. The only hope was to keep the flames from spreading to the stables.

But Blake had little thought for these details. He and Walmsley were making their way towards the solitary figure of the woman in black who stood gaunt and silent in the glare of the flames, gazing at them with a hard, enigmatic expression.

She turned as they approached, and, after a searching look at Blake, kept her eyes fixed on Walmsley. Blake gave the latter a nudge, and, when they paused beside her, Walmsley said quietly:

"Are you willing to tell us anything, ma'am? You may know who I am. I knew Junius Markheim well, and I was here yesterday. If you are willing to help us with any information I can assure you you have nothing to fear. This gentleman is Mr. Sexton Blake, a well-known detective. Will you say anything?"

She swept a sharp look back at Blake, then turned a stony gaze on Walmsley.

"I have nothing to say. I know you, Romer Walmsley. You would still be in there among those flames if it weren't for me."

"It was you who set me free. I thought as much."

"It was nothing to me what happened to you. I set you free thinking you would return in time to rescue the girl. But you have come too late. Junius Markheim has been too clever for you once more. He will never be caught now. He is gone with the girl and another."

"Carlotta?"

"Who else?"

"But, ma'am, there were others in the house —two men who came to see Markheim to-night."

"You will find their remains among the ashes. Junius strikes with certainty. Ask me no more. I am Junius Markheim's wife. Tell your police to arrest me if they wish."

Walmsley would have said something more, but Blake warned him with a sharp nudge.

He had realised all of a sudden that there was a wealth of mystery behind this woman in black that must be probed, and he knew that, despite her apparent enmity towards the police, she bore a far more deadly grudge against Markheim.

If he could only get hold of that and turn it to his own purpose; if he could reach out and lay hands on Markheim as surely as he knew this gaunt creature in black would stretch her hand into the mist of his retreat and pluck him from it! For he knew that, in some way, she would do so. In that stony woman was housed the Nemesis that crouched in wait for Junius Markheim.

But why hadn't she struck before? Blake could find no answer to that question.

Chapter 16. Mr. Markheim Speaks.

THE pursuit of Markheim could only be a half-hearted attempt at best.

By the time the police car was swung round and a definite decision come to, the fugitive was well up the valley. Cramer volunteered to tackle the job, and Lethbridge, knowing how keen he was now to make a mark in the case, agreed quickly. With but one other man —the police chauffeur —they went off, but Blake expected little result.

As for himself and Walmsley, there could be no question yet of returning to London. Naturally they wanted to see what could be discovered when the wreckage of the burning mansion would allow a search to be made. But, more than anything else, Blake wanted to keep near the woman in black.

Mrs. Markheim!

He could well believe it. And he could guess something of the story that must lie behind the tragedy of her life. Had she, as a young woman of some attraction, married Markheim believing him to be honest? Or had she done so knowing him to be a crook? That was a question he could never answer unless she enlightened him.

But from what Walmsley was able to tell him, what he remembered of the shadowy figure that had stood in the background in South America, and her own confession that it was she who had given Walmsley his freedom, he could piece together some of the story as it must have been unfolded.

There could be no doubt that the woman Carlotta had figured as a strong factor in the affair, Walmsley had painted her as an exotic creature of the South who was a fitting mate for Markheim in any form of devilry he might undertake. Had she supplanted the woman in black? Was jealousy of Carlotta the mainspring of her motive in releasing Walmsley? Or was she jealous of Julia de Santos? Or, again, were there many others of her sex of whom she had had reason to feel deep hatred? Did she still love Markheim? If so, why had she remained behind when he fled?

There was mystery here, Blake knew. And his well-trained detective faculties told him that through the woman in black lay the road to Markheim's discovery, if such existed. If Markheim had driven off into the night without any definite objective in view other than escape from the immediate danger that threatened him, then there was a good chance of Cramer picking up his trail sooner or later.

But if he had a bolt-hole prepared, as he had prepared this place, then was it not possible that the woman in black would know of its existence and location? Studying that gaunt, face and those stony eyes, Blake could not but believe that she must have known most of the details of Markheim's affairs, whether with his consent or not. She was not the type that could be left out of consideration.

It followed as a matter of course that Lethbridge should place her under formal arrest as soon as he learned that she was Markheim's wife. The woman seemed scarcely to heed the few words that warned her of her fate. She listened until he had finished, then she turned and walked towards the stable, not waiting to see if she were to be placed under guard.

Lethbridge was standing in a hesitant way, as if uncertain just what to do. Blake intervened at this point, saying: "Will you leave her to me, Lethbridge? I'll be responsible for her. I don't think you will be able to make any case against her in any event."

"Who is she, anyway?"

"Markheim's wife —she says."

"We can't force her to give evidence against him, but she was probably mixed up in his crook games."

"You'll never prove it. What evidence there may exist has gone either to destruction in those flames or is in Markheim's possession. I shall see that she is ready to be produced when you want her."

"Have your way, Blake," responded the inspector, with a shrug.

Blake drew Walmsley aside.

"I'm going to try and get her to talk, Walmsley. You had better leave us alone. I suggest that you remain here and watch out for any signs of the two French crooks. They may not have been in the house. It is quite on the cards that Markheim popped them into some place that remains to be discovered. Or he may have taken them away with him."

Walmsley rejoined Lethbridge, and Blake walked slowly along to the stable through a side door of which the woman in black had disappeared. He found her in a small harness-room that looked as if it had been used as a sort of lounging-place for some of Markheim's men, for it contained a battered horsehair-covered settee, and a couple of chairs.

The woman had switched on an electric light, and was silting on the couch, her arms crossed, and her stony gaze fixed on the floor. She did not even look up as Blake entered, but that she had recognised him was obvious, for she said tonelessly:

"You needn't be afraid that I shall try to escape. I don't care what they do with me."

"I haven't come as a police guard," answered Blake quietly. "I have asked the inspector to allow you as much liberty as possible. But I thought you might be inclined to talk with me, Mrs. Markheim, when I assure you that I only seek to find your husband in order to rescue Julia de Santos and recover her property. I would like to tell you how I happened to come into this affair —in a way quite independent of the police. Will you listen?"

"I can't stop you from talking," was the ungracious reply.

Blake sat down in one of the stiff chairs, and, asking permission, lit a cigarette. Then he began to speak, casually, conversationally, telling her how Walmsley had come to him on his arrival in England to ask his aid in running down Junius Markheim; told her how he had refused because he would be no party to a vendetta of the sort Walmsley was suggesting; explained how Walmsley had returned to him after she had made it possible for him to escape, and then how Scotland Yard had become interested in Markheim through his negotiations with Benoit and Acier.

"I can assure, you that neither I nor Mr. Walmsley will interfere in your relations with your husband," he went on in the same level tones when the woman deigned no comment. "What caused him to get in touch with Benoit and Acier I can guess. I know the record of both those men. They had no intention of paying your husband any money for the De Santos gems. He made a serious mistake there, as you must know now. But I have committed myself now to the recovery of those gems and the rescue of Miss de Santos. I have nothing to do with Junius Markheim beyond that. It is for the police. What may have passed between your husband and the two Frenchmen I do not know. You could probably enlighten me, if you wished, as to their fate. If their remains are found among those ruins then Junius Markheim has a difficult explanation to make. But, again, I say —that is for the police. I do not think you have been a happy woman, Mrs. Markheim. I do not know what sentiments you hold against your husband. But I want you to know just where I stand in this. You may not know anything about me, but if you will take the trouble to make inquiries you will find that I have some reputation for keeping my word. And I do promise you that if you will help me in this thing I will do my best for you. If you prefer to say nothing, you can, of course, adopt that course. But I, and I know I can speak for Mr. Walmsley as well, wish to be your friend. Think over what I have said. You may need someone to advise you before this business is done with."

His voice died away, and he sat smoking in silence. The woman moved her position a little, interlinking her two hands across one knee. Yet she did not speak. Silence reigned, broken only by the distant sounds in the grounds.

Minutes passed, and Blake did not make any further attempt to press his point. He knew he could say nothing more to influence her, and he told himself that she might be ruled entirely by loyalty to Markheim. If that were the case then he must confess his instinct wrong. And, further, he would have to find some other explanation of her release of Walmsley with the charge to return and rescue Julia de Santos.

But, suddenly, she spoke. Her voice was lower pitched than Blake's had been, and even more toneless. There was a something desolate in it that affected Blake keenly, hardened though he was to human suffering.

"I know more about you than you think I do," he heard her saying. "But you can only guess things about me. You are a shrewd man. That is what is said about you, and you have proved it tonight. You said you did not believe I had been a very happy woman. Dear Heaven!"

She broke into a laugh that reeked with bitterness and disillusion.

"Happy! I have not known the meaning of the word for twenty years. I have only known a consuming hatred and desire for vengeance. You assure me that you wish Junius Markheim no harm. As if that mattered. No one shall take from me my right to wreak upon him the punishment he deserves. For twenty years he has outraged everything that should have been sacred between us. For twenty years I have stood in the shadow behind him and watched his schemes. For twenty years I have counted the procession of other women who have filled his interest for a time, only to be cast aside when he had no further use for them. But I have bided my time. I knew that the time would come when I could repay him to the full. I knew that Junius Markheim would climb high. He is that sort. Few men can match his brains; few men could sink to such depths of cruelty. He is strong and cunning and without soul.

"I knew why he never came to England. I knew it was because he was keeping this country as the one place to which he could retire in safety. And I waited, waited for the moment when he would be on the top of the mountain he had set himself to climb before I hurled him down. Happy! And now you come to me and talk of rescuing Julia de Santos. He would have had legal possession of her jewels long ago had I not prevented it —he and the creature with the macaw. What think you I care for the police? I have done no wrong. They cannot force me to give evidence. They may keep me for a while, but they must let me go. And I am in no haste. It is better to wait until Junius Markheim feels himself safe again. The police will get no help from me. I wait only until the time comes, and then I seize the moment that has been snatched from me this night."

Blake had listened from beginning to end without betraying the slightest outward sign of interest. So swiftly did the story come, so unrestrained did the words tumble from the woman's lips, that he knew he was receiving the full volume of what had been bottled up for twenty years. It was probably the first time that this sombre, suffering woman had let down the bars of her restraint, and he could not attempt to guess why she had elected to do so with him this night.

He could only think it might be because the shock of what had happened had for the moment breached the wall of her long silence. And he knew he must tread very warily if he were to turn the confession to his own advantage.

For he believed her. He could picture the dreary years during which her youth and charm and hopes had been beaten flat under the colossal selfishness and brutality of Junius Markheim. He could understand how she had frozen more and more each year until but one spark remained within her, a spark that had glowed beneath an ever-growing heap of fuel, to burst into flame when the moment came. And he had a world of sympathy with her.

He knew that she did not exaggerate when she said that the woman, Carlotta, was but one of the long stream of women who had passed across the line of Junius Markheim's life. The big crook was just the type to turn such women to his purposes and discard them when he had no further use for them. Whether she still possessed any love for Markheim was beyond his conception, or, in fact, beyond that of any mere man.

A woman's mind works in such a complicated manner that this gaunt creature in black might be burning to destroy the man through love or through an undying hatred. Who could tell?

"It would be idle for me to tell you how much I appreciate your confidence," he said quietly at last. "And I can understand the motive that governs you. But, forgive me, if you refuse to help the police, how do you expect to achieve your purpose? Surely exposure, arrest and conviction would be the greatest ruin that could overtake the man."

"I have my own plans. Let him realise his wealth or let him feel that he is entirely safe. Then I shall deal with him and the woman."

"But what about Miss de Santos? Are you going to leave that helpless girl in his power?"

"I gave Walmsley a chance. He failed. Why should I worry now?"

"No reason, I suppose, except that you might have had a daughter just about that age yourself, and you would not want her to be in the power of a man such as Junius Markheim has proved himself to be."

She was silent then. All unknowing, Blake had struck very deep. Bitterest of all her thoughts was that she had no children. Had she possessed such a daughter as Julia de Santos it is possible that her consuming desire for vengeance would have found outlet in milder channels. There was an odd change in her voice when she spoke again, a tinge of feeling that gave it an almost sweet timbre.

"What could be done now to rescue the girl without the police knowing?"

Blake turned his head and gazed into the dark, burning eyes.

"I will tell you what I think," he said gently. "I am sure you must know where Junius Markheim has betaken himself. If I were you I would go to him and inform him that he must receive Mr. Walmsley and me. Assure him that the police do not know his whereabouts, but that you have revealed them to me. Tell him that his only hope of escape is to accede to your terms.

"Make those terms a condition that he gives up the woman Carlotta. I'll agree to a period of twenty-four hours in which he can escape if possible. And I will bind myself not to inform the police until after I have seen him. That will be a test. If he plays fair by you and us he will get his twenty-four hours, though I will be frank with you and say that I consider his chances of escape as very small.

"On the other hand, he may be able to make a good case of self-defence against the two French crooks if they have perished in the fire. If he plays treacherous then we should have to be ready. But in this way you will get another chance to achieve your end without bringing in the police.

"But they must come in eventually. You will see that. This is England, not South America. I am advising you as honestly as I can, and if you make this agreement with me I pledge you my word I shall not betray your confidence. Think of that helpless girl if of nothing else."

He finished. He had said all he could. He knew that to go beyond that might be to ruin it all. It now lay with her and depended on how she reacted to his plea.

For a good ten minutes or so they sat in a new silence. Blake did not look at her again —just lit a fresh cigarette and stared at the floor. But at last she stirred, and he heard her say:

"I'm going to trust you. I swore I should never again trust man or woman. But I believe you are straight. I will tell you where to find Junius Markheim. You will not have far to go. At this moment he is within three miles of this spot, and that is why the police will never trace him unless they are led to him."

Chapter 17. Blake's Bargain.

IT was about twenty minutes later that Blake left the woman in black and made his way out to where the others were gathered watching the final dissolution of the house.

A village fire brigade had arrived on the scene with an antiquated pumping engine that needed a dozen men to work the parallel pumping-bars up and down. A length of hose had been run into a pond about a hundred yards away, but the jerky stream of water that was sent spurting into the flaming skeleton of the mansion might as well have been dispensed with, of so little avail was it.

Blake got hold of Lethbridge and took him to one side, signing to Walmsley that he would talk with him presently.

"Look here, Lethbridge," he said when they were out of earshot, "I've had a bit of a talk with the woman in black. There is no doubt that she is Mrs. Markheim, and I can assure you it will be a mistake to arrest her. I am prepared to state emphatically that she has had no part in whatever hanky-panky Markheim has been up to. She has lived on his support, it is true; but you can't prosecute her for that. Nor can you force her to give evidence against him."

"That may be, Blake, but she is the only one of any consequence we have grabbed out of the bunch. I don't count the dagoes we found in the stable loft."

"Wait a minute, Lethbridge. You know me too well to think that I would allow you to risk letting anyone of importance get away. But if you will be guided by me in this I believe you will get vastly more out of her than if you rouse her hostility.

"I have been told some things in confidence that I am not at liberty yet to reveal. But I wish you would reconsider matters. If you will leave her in my care I am prepared to be responsible for her.

"You started to find out what the two French crooks were up to. Their remains may be found among those ruins or they may not. They may have got away with Markheim, but from what I have heard from the woman I am inclined to think they will be found to have perished in the fire. If they were double-crossing Markheim, then that will come out when we learn more. But my chief aim is to get in touch with a young woman whom he took away in his flight. I won't interfere in your business, but I think if you will be guided by me in this I can give you a hint as to where to find Markheim sooner than

94

you will learn it elsewhere."

"We'll find him all right."

"Possibly. But it isn't going to be easy. I am not talking moonshine. Will you stay your hand and leave Mrs. Markheim to me? I will produce her when you want her. And it is going to be better for you to have her as a willing aid than a hostile witness."

Lethbridge nodded after a pause.

"You can have her. But I hold you to your promise. I'd like to settle this before Thomas returns from the north and I don't mind telling you I'm anxious for Cramer to make a showing."

"Neither he nor you will lose if it has anything to do with me."

Blake joined Walmsley a few moments later and led him towards the stables. He told him, more or less, what had passed between him and Mrs. Markheim and, as he proceeded with the story, Walmsley kept nodding in agreement.

"That explains it," he said when Blake had finished. "She must be a sticker. Fancy her bluffing Markheim all these years. She must have had him afraid of her. He would have killed off anyone else. But do you think she is kidding when she says she will lead us to him?"

"I'm gambling on her having told the truth. But mind, Walmsley, not a word to Lethbridge. I've pledged myself."

"What is your plan?"

"I'm going to trust her alone. I've got to. If she lets me down it will put me in a bad hole with Lethbridge, but I have a hunch she will play straight. I'm going to get her into my car and drive her some distance on the road to where Markheim has gone to earth. Then we'll leave her and to-morrow evening, after we learn more about what is found among the ruins of the house, we will make a call on Markheim. With the police net out in every direction he will lie low for a bit."

"But do you think she told the truth when she said he was only about three miles away?"

"It was that statement that sounded more convincing than anything else. It is just the sort of thing a shrewd crook like Markheim would have fixed. Who would think that he had a second bolthole ready to pop into so close to this? It is a master-stroke of strategy."

"I believe you are right. Well, I am entirely in your hands. All I want to do is to get Julia de Santos out of that devil's hands. If what Mrs. Markheim says is right, then it is only she who has prevented

Markheim and Carlotta working their will with her. Take it from me, if she stands out against them now, Junius Markheim will kill her. Carlotta will stand in on that. She isn't squeamish."

"I agree. And Markheim won't want himself burdened with any extra weight, so to say, when he makes his next dash. He may think his wife perished in the fire. She seems to have some reason for believing he will get such an idea. But I don't fear for her. She will be able to hold her own. And she is the link we have to depend on, Walmsley. Now if you will get the car ready I will bring her along. I'll just give Lethbridge a word to say that I am taking her to a place where she can spend the night."

If the woman in black felt any regret at the confidence she had reposed in Blake she gave no sign of it. When he reentered the harness room she was still sitting just as he had left her, staring stonily at the floor. He told her what arrangement he had made with the inspector.

"I've given my parole on your behalf, Mrs. Markheim," he said quietly. "I'm going to keep faith with you and I believe you will keep faith with me. I want you to know that I will do whatever I can to help you."

She rose and fixed her dark eyes on him.

"Give me your hand," she said curtly.

He obeyed. Her thin fingers tightened on his convulsively and her voice once more betrayed a hint of emotion as she said:

"I have promised. I trust you. I will not betray you. What do you wish me to do?"

"I am going to take you to that other place, or near it, if you wish to go. The car is ready."

"And leave me there?"

"Mr. Walmsley and I will remain close at hand for your protection if you desire it."

She made a gesture of scorn.

"I have no fear of Junius Markheim or the creature, Carlotta. I will go with you. Before we get there I will tell you what you are to do."

Blake took the wheel of the Grey Panther with Mrs. Markheim beside him. Walmsley got into the back. Once they were out of the grounds (the police had got the big gates open and kept them wide) he drove down the hill, across the little stone bridge and along the valley road to the main highway.

He gathered from what she said that, while she could find her way to the place that was their objective on foot across the paddocks —she had trailed Markheim more than once to the spot —she was uncertain just how they should go by road. But with a rough description of the location Blake took a chance on finding it by turning off to the left at the first cross roads they came to. He carried on about a couple of miles in this direction until they saw a narrow, little used turning again on the left.

The woman seemed convinced that this would take them to the house and Blake decided it would be safer to go ahead on foot, for it was quite on the cards that Markheim would be on the qui vive and would be suspicious if he saw motor lights approaching.

He left Walmsley with the Grey Panther and walked into the dark road with the woman. They carried on for a quarter of a mile or so when suddenly she stopped and grasped his arm.

"Do you see something that looks like a stile on the left?" she whispered.

"Wait here. I see what you mean."

He crossed a shallow ditch and found that what was a faint skeleton, was, as she had thought, a stile. He returned to confirm it.

"I remember crossing that. The house is only a quarter of a mile or so farther along. There are no others near it. It is a red brick building much smaller than the other —some distance in off the road. There is no lodge. Come there at nine o'clock to-morrow evening and you will find Junius Markheim. I shall see that he does not get away before then."

"I will come. You will keep faith?"

"I will keep faith."

With that he stepped away and waited while her figure faded away into the gloom beyond. When he could no longer see her or hear the faint sound of her footsteps he turned and strode back to the car.

For the rest of that night Blake and Walmsley dozed in one of the hay lofts above the stable. There was nothing they could do to assist at the fire which was, by now, reduced to a glowing mass of smoking embers. It would be some hours before it would be possible to get in among the ruins to make a search and they wanted to be on hand to see what was found.

When they turned out a little after six in the morning they found that Cramer had returned to report no luck in his pursuit of Markheim. Nor had he been able to get any traces of such a van having been seen passing through any of the nearby towns and villages, either on the road to London or towards the coast; a piece of news which did not surprise Blake considering that, if what the woman in black had said was true, Markheim would be 'smoked' away almost within rifle shot of where they stood.

When it was certain that several hours more must elapse before a search could be begun, Blake decided to run up to London to attend to some business, taking Walmsley with him. Lethbridge did not press him to say where he had left Mrs. Markheim nor did Blake reopen the subject.

It was four o'clock in the afternoon when he again drove the Grey Panther into the grounds of the ruined mansion. By this time a good many inquisitive persons had collected and the search of the ruins was in full swing. Lethbridge had begun his investigations at the spot where the front hall had been and, penetrating from there, was able to pick up the location of the library easily enough through the mass of molten metal that had formed the steel barricade to the door and a great lump of glass that they knew was what remained of the heavy plate-glass barrier that had divided the room at Markheim's will.

They came upon all sorts of iron remains, small girders, slabs of cement and so on which they were able, gradually, to identify as part and parcel of a complicated system of secret gadgets which they knew now that Markheim had employed.

But the most interesting item was the remains of a big shaft which was brought to light just before six o'clock and which was at first believed to be the remains of a lift. But when the debris had been cleared away they came upon the big steel safe, still very hot but quite intact. Outwardly it had withstood the fierce heat in a way that did credit to its makers.

Other parties were engaged in raking over different sections of the ruins in the search for human bones, for it was still believed possible that someone might have been on the upper floor when the roof collapsed. Not a single thing was found, however, to support this theory. But about seven o'clock when the safe was finally got open, a discovery was made which solved one mystery that had been puzzling Blake and Walmsley as well as Lethbridge and Cramer.

Inside, lying just as they had been tumbled, were the bodies of Benoit and "Acier." They had been roasted to a cinder, for the heat inside the steel safe must have been terrific for hours. Yet it was easy enough to identify them and, after a brief examination, Blake turned away. He was glad of the approach of the hour when he and Walmsley must keep their appointment with the woman in black.

It was still comparatively light when they once more took the road along which they had driven the night before. As they approached the spot where Blake and Mrs. Markheim had got out, Blake slowed down to find a quiet parking place, for they could not tell what had developed since the woman's appearance. Blake knew he had been taking a big gamble in trusting to her to keep Markheim there, but there had been something in her calm assurance that had impressed him.

It was Walmsley who spotted an open gate with a big haystack near at hand, such as that behind which he had hidden his motor-cycle on the occasion of his first visit to Markheim. Blake turned the car in and manoeuvred round so it was facing again towards the gate. It were as well to be prepared for a quick getaway.

Then they got out and went ahead on foot, each making sure that his automatic was ready to hand, for they knew enough after seeing what remained of the two French crooks to realise that, having gone the whole hog in one direction, Junius Markheim would not hesitate to continue to kill if his safety demanded it.

Chapter 18.   Closing in on the Crooks.

DUSK was beginning to close in when they saw, through the trees, the red brick house which they knew must be their objective.

It was a cosy, homely house of medium size —a place such as a modestly prosperous merchant might retire to, or a retreat eagerly snapped up by a retired Anglo-Indian. With its well-kept grounds and its highly respectable façade, it was the last place one would select as the bolthole of a crook of Junius Markheim's calibre.

They made no attempt to conceal their approach. If the woman in black had done her work then they would be expected. And they had to trust to her that they were not shot down in their tracks as they strode up the drive.

Blake had been unable to form any definite plan of conduct. Until he saw Markheim's attitude he must keep an open mind. But as soon as Markheim showed his hand, then he would act accordingly. He had just two objects —to secure the release of Julia de Santos and to recover a good portion, at least, of her jewels. In return, he had to offer Markheim what must count as a thing of great value —a twenty-four hours start before the police hounds were in full cry.

On the other hand, Blake knew perfectly well that he and Walmsley were carrying their lives in their hands from the moment they entered the gate and started up that neatly-edged drive. He knew that Markheim might count the risk of a double murder worth while rather than submit to terms which would cramp him severely.

He would gain as much of a start, or even more, possibly, by killing Walmsley and Blake than if he made terms. But there was to be weighed against that the loophole of defence he could put up against a capital charge in the case of Benoit and "Acier"; whereas he wouldn't have the shred of a chance if charged with the murder of Blake and Walmsley.

It was to be a tricky time, and none knew it better than Blake. Not a sign came from the blank face of the house as they drew closer. Not a light showed to proclaim the presence of anyone within. Yet they had an uneasy feeling that their every step was being watched by invisible eyes.

They mounted the porch steps without pausing. Blake pressed the button on the left of the green-painted door and stood back a little, on guard. Almost at once they could hear subdued movements within,

100

then came a slight rattling as the handle was turned and the door pulled open. Staring at them was Jose.

No flicker of recognition passed between him and the visitors. They might never have met so impersonal was his scrutiny. Yet not forty-eight hours before he had led a murderous attack on Walmsley, and less than twenty-four hours had passed since he had tried desperately to knife Blake.

"We have come to see your master," said Blake, first in English, then, as Jose continued to stare stupidly, in Spanish.

Jose stood back and drew the door wider.

"Enter, senores," he said curtly. "You are expected."

It seemed too easy. For the fraction of a moment Blake hesitated before crossing the threshold. Despite the many desperate situations in which he had been involved in his long, adventurous career, a slight shiver ran down his spine as he put away his hesitancy and passed into the dim hall.

Jose waited until Walmsley had followed, then he closed the door and, with a muttered word, preceded them along the hall to a door on the right. Opening this, he passed inside, and spoke to someone whom the visitors could not see.

"Two senores have come, senor."

Came a guttural voice bidding him request them to enter. They had no need to wonder to whom those tones belonged. Walmsley knew them well enough, and Blake had no difficulty in guessing.

There was no hesitancy in Blake's manner now. With the crisis reached he was only too eager to get to grips. He stepped over the threshold and came into a long, low-ceilinged room that was the quintessence of repose and good taste. He guessed correctly that Markheim had bought the place, lock, stock and barrel.

It was a lounge sitting-room in type, with a black polished floor, deep, chintz-covered chairs and couches, many pieces of old oak, and, dominating all, a gem of a long refectory table some distance down on the left.

At this table, his back to the wall, was the huge bulk of a man. It was Junius Markheim. But the burly crook was not the only occupant of the room when they entered. Farther along, at the end of the table, was a sombre figure which was scarcely discernible in the light of the two candles which burned in tall silver sconces, one at each end of the dark, oak board. It was the woman in black. But of Carlotta or Julia de

Santos or the macaw there was no sign.

In deference, apparently, to the sultry evening, one of the low windows was open, the curtains moving listlessly in the faint current of air that found its way in. This window was exactly opposite the table at which Markheim sat, and as the draught stirred the flames of the candles little waves of shadow passed across his heavy cheeks, giving him a sinister expression which is as often seen on the countenance of a fat man as on that of a thin man, despite the popular belief to the contrary.

Opposite him, too, was a long, leather-padded, oaken settee, to which, after one searching glance at his visitors, he waved a hand.

"Sit down," he ordered rather than invited.

Blake did not hesitate. He was willing to wait until Markheim "pulled the string," so to say. He bowed slightly to the woman in black and pushed along between the settle and the table, followed by Walmsley, seating himself directly opposite Markheim; Walmsley was on his left, facing an empty chair, the purpose of which they were to learn presently.

For the space of a full half-minute the eyes of the crook and those of the detective remained fixed together. Then Markheim lifted one great hand and let it fall on the oak with a soft thud.

"Well, Mr. Sexton Blake, what do you want?" He ignored Walmsley utterly.

"That, I think, is known to you," answered Blake coldly. "If you wish, I shall put it into words."

"I do wish."

"I want the person of one Julia de Santos, and I want certain property in the form of jewels belonging to her. I have one offer to make in return."

"Which is?"

"That from midnight to-night you get twenty-four hours' grace before the police are given definite information as to where you are in hiding."

"And if I refuse?"

"They will be informed as soon as I get in touch with them."

"You seem confident that you will be able to return to them," remarked the crook, with a heavy sneer.

"Of course. I have no uncertainty on that score, Mr. Markheim."

Markheim's eyes flashed to the sombre figure at the end of the table. In the slanting light of the candle Blake saw such a look of venomous hatred in the pale eyes as to cause him to stiffen. He would not have been surprised had Markheim hurled himself upon her and closed his great fingers on her throat. But she stared back at him unwinkingly, as composed as if she were present at an ordinary business conference and nothing more.

Markheim brought his gaze back to Blake.

"There is no need for me to disguise the relationship that exists between me and this woman," he said at last. "She has informed me of her conversation with you. I care not two straws for the police. They have no charge against me."

"You are mistaken," broke in Blake coolly. "They have a charge of double murder against you, Markheim. The bodies of Benoit and Acier were found this afternoon."

A tiny indication of change showed in Markheim's eyes for a moment, but his voice was even as he rejoined:

"This is nothing. I acted in self-defence. They were a pair of crooks who tried first to swindle me and then to shoot me. I got them first, that is all."

"I don't dispute that. You may not find it easy to convince the police. And you will find it even more difficult to explain why you are holding the person of Miss de Santos as well as what right you have to dispose of her jewels. That was your business with Benoit and Acier. I am surprised that one of your undoubted discrimination did not guess they were crooks."

Markheim's face definitely flushed at the taunt, but he still kept his voice under control. Blake glanced towards the woman in black and seemed to sense that she was trying to flash him a warning of some sort. He could not fathom its exact meaning, but it put him more than ever on his guard.

"We shall discuss the purpose of your visit. You have taken into account, I presume, the risk you ran in coming here?"

"Naturally. I am not so callow as to ignore that."

"Yet you are at my mercy."

"You would be unwise to dwell on that or to act on that belief."

"I do what I think best. But this rubbish you have brought with you—" indicating Walmsley — "it amuses me to see him posing as a champion of the defenceless. Has he told you what part he played in getting possession of the jewels of which you speak?"

"Yes; and of the part you played in the killing of old man De Santos. But we will not discuss Mr. Walmsley's part in this. He has put himself in my hands. I am determined to see justice done to Miss de Santos, so let us stop beating about the bush, Markheim."

"Very well. What would you say if I showed you a proper conveyance from Miss de Santos to me of the jewels of which you speak?"

"I should say you had secured it by force, threats or trickery."

"Indeed. And if you were to hear from the girl's own lips that she gave it of her own free will and accord? That she is quite happy with me and does not desire to make any change?"

"I should still say you had employed illicit means."

"Nevertheless, you shall see with your own eyes and hear with your own ears. But before I send for her let me say something. I know what passed between you and this woman, who, unfortunately, is my wife. I know how she has betrayed me. I can guess her motive. I shall deal with her later. But I warn you now that after I have convinced you that Miss de Santos is not held under any restraint and that she has given me a power of attorney to act on her behalf, you do not clear out, I shall take whatever measures seem best for my own protection and at my own risk."

"I shall not leave without the girl and her property," answered Blake coldly.

"So be it. Take my terms."

With that, Markheim turned to the woman.

"Bring them." he ordered curtly.

She rose, and, in passing, Blake thought she once more gave him a meaning look. He knew that things were fast approaching a crisis and that he would need to be on guard every moment. He could not tell yet whether Markheim was bluffing or not, but he had an instinct that he was about to play his last hand and that he had it packed with strong cards.

He waited tensely, pushing one foot along to signal a warning to Walmsley. As they sat he knew he could whip out his weapon and cover Markheim, but he did not know what that would avail. It was impossible to tell what he had done with Julia de Santos. He might only be bluffing and playing for time. The girl might not be in the house at all.

But a few moments later Blake found that she was indeed

present, for the door opened and out of the penumbra of light came two forms. One was the exotic, flaming creature Carlotta, with the brilliantly hued macaw on her shoulder; the other was a girl whose loveliness was undeniable.

Dark as Carlotta she was, but in a different way. Her face was, however, but a lifeless mask for all its beauty, her eyes lacklustre and staring as she walked slowly towards the table. She was dressed all in soft white with a single red flower at her bosom, the only other touch of contrasting colour being a small black silk mantilla that was drawn about her dark hair.

Markheim rose clumsily and smiled at her.

"Come, Julia, my dear, only for a few moments. Sit here. I want you to answer one or two questions."

She did not answer but allowed Carlotta to guide her to the chair into which she sank listlessly. Carlotta took the other chair, her black eyes sweeping Blake and Walmsley mockingly. The woman in black had not returned. There was some devilry afloat, that was certain.

Blake had been watching the girl. It was obvious that she was moving under some strong hypnotic influence, either human or drug. He was scientist enough to know the meaning of those distended pupils and the purely automatic muscular movements.

He had risen as had Walmsley, and she had responded with a little inclination of the head when they bowed. But now, as Markheim resumed his seat and spoke, she turned her lovely eyes on him. Blake heard Walmsley exhale sharply, but his attention was all for Markheim.

"Senorita Julia," he was saying in a voice as caressing as he could make it, and yet, with a quiver of command running through it, "Senorita Julia, these senores have come to ascertain if you are quite happy with me and Senorita Carlotta, Will you answer them please? You are happy —is it not so?"

She did not remove her eyes from his as she answered.

"Happy —oh, yes, quite happy."

"You do not wish to be taken away from our care?"

She shivered and moved closer to Carlotta, who smiled evilly above her head.

"Oh, no! I do not wish to go away. You must not allow me to do so."

"And certain jewels which I am taking care of on your behalf —

you do not wish anyone to handle them?"

"No, senor —only you."

"You signed a paper —do you remember?"

"Si, senor."

"It was an authority for me to act for you. You still wish me to do so?"

"But yes, senor."

"And what do you wish these gentlemen to do?"

"Send them away, senor. I do not know them."

"You are perfectly happy and content?"

"Perfectly, senor."

"Enough of this farce."

It was Blake who interrupted. Carlotta gave him a venomous look and her black eyes glittered with deep hate. Markheim turned to him with a frown.

"What do you mean? You have heard and seen. Is that not enough? Is it not what I promised?"

"Don't take us for children, Markheim. The girl is speaking and moving under an influence. You cannot convince me. It is all a sheer waste of time. I repeat the demand I made when I came. Hand over Miss de Santos and her property and I will keep my word. Refuse, and we shall take her anyway, and you will be closed up here like a rat in its hole."

Markheim banged his fist on the heavy oak. He did not speak. He did not have to do so. Carlotta gave vent to a low, sharp cry at the same moment, and instinctively Sexton Blake knew it was a signal of some sort. It was a sudden slant of Markheim's eyes that warned him. There flashed into his mind the thought that all this time he and Walmsley had been sitting with their backs to the open window. He sensed treachery, and on the very moment when he caught the sudden signalling gleam in Markheim's eyes he shouted to Walmsley and threw himself to one side, dragging out his automatic as he did so.

The upheaval was appalling.

A few moments before the room had been in comparative calm. What had taken place had been orderly enough. No voices had been upraised. No sign of commotion until now, and, echoing Blake's shout, came a warning scream from the gloom at the far end of the room.

What instinct sent him swaying to one side Blake never could tell. But while he had his automatic only half out of his pocket, he was held frozen in horrified amazement at what he saw.

Something flashed past his check so close as to leave the breath of its passage; something stuck quivering in Junius Markheim's fat throat in almost the same instant, and sent him to his feet with a hoarse yell of terror, while a wild scream burst from the lips of Carlotta.

Like one in a fit of uncontrollable frenzy, she leaped from her chair, her screams aimed in incoherent words towards the open window. The macaw, which until then had been quiet enough, joined its screeches with hers, and, taking wing, began swooping about like a mad thing, tearing at Walmsley with talons and scimitar beak.

From somewhere Carlotta threw up a pistol and aimed it full at Blake. Her finger was in the very act of flexing on the trigger and Blake instinctively threw himself back, while he strove to get his own weapon into play. But before he could do so, even while Carlotta's finger dragged back and the pistol barked, there was another crash of sound in the room, and while Blake was conscious that a bullet had seared his arm, he saw a burst of crimson at the side of Carlotta's throat. A choking gurgle came from between her lips, she reeled and faced Junius Markheim, who was still clawing madly at the thing that stuck in his throat; then the pair faced each other full for the fraction of a second before crashing to the floor as one. In the same instant Julia de Santos slid to the floor in a dead faint, while out of the gloom came the woman in black, a still smoking pistol hanging loosely in her right hand.

She laid the weapon on the table and knelt at once over the unconscious Julia.

She paid not the slightest attention either to the dead man and woman, nor to Blake and Walmsley. As for Blake, after the first spasm of amazed paralysis passed, he swung and gazed towards the window. Both he and Walmsley knew well enough what it was that had pierced Markheim in the throat, and why it had killed him so quickly. There is no poison that acts more swiftly than the venom used by the Indians of South America on the tips of their poisoned darts. But they knew, too, that it had been intended for Blake, and only his swift action had saved him.

"Go and see, Walmsley. Watch out, the murderer may be lying in wait."

Walmsley drew his pistol and strode to the window. Leaping over the sill he stood peering through the heavy dusk into the garden. Blake was already bending over Markheim, but he knew he was past help. And he knew it was equally useless to attempt to succour Carlotta. Rising, he hurried to the window as he heard Walmsley calling. He jumped into the garden and half-ran to the spot where the other was bending over something on the ground. When he reached the spot he saw it was a huddled human form, and then he recognised the mestizo, Jose. Beside him was a long, slender bamboo blowpipe. It was easy enough to guess now who had sent that tiny messenger of death through the open window. And, gripped between the thumb and first finger of one hand was another little dart, the poisoned tip close to his naked throat where a short scar showed how he had scratched the fatal wound.

"I wonder why he did it?" muttered Walmsley.

"That dart was intended for you," responded Blake, in a low tone. "When he saw how the first one missed its mark and struck his master in the throat, he cared for nothing but to follow Markheim's spirit as quickly as possible. He knew it must kill; he knew he must make haste if he were to overtake Markheim in the spirit world before he got lost among the forests there. I think, if we knew the truth, Walmsley, we should find that Markheim and Jose were blood-brothers. It would explain a lot. Jose may be a mestizo, but I'll warrant he had a lot of Arawakan blood in him, and that is the belief of that tribe. It would explain a lot of other things, too."

They straightened up and gazed towards the house, where they could see Mrs. Markheim moving against the candle-light.

"She saved your life, Blake," remarked Walmsley thoughtfully.

The detective nodded.

"She did. I didn't know she was at the other end of the room. If the poisoned dart had got me first, Carlotta would have shot you dead, Walmsley. She and Markheim had it all planned that we were not to leave here alive unless we swallowed his bluff. Let us go in. There are some things that must be said between us and that strange woman there. Whatever comes, she stands clear after what has happened here to-night. I shall get you to endorse my statement that she shot Carlotta to save my life. It was a close shave for both of us, but as things have turned out I can't help but think it is for the best."

His companion nodded, and together they returned to the window and climbed over the low sill.

     •   •   •   •   •

Needless to say, Inspector Lethbridge was a good deal surprised and, it must be confessed, a little nettled, when Blake returned to inform him that not only had he found Markheim, but that he was dead. However, when Blake insisted that his name be kept out of it, and that Lethbridge should handle the whole matter, he was inclined to look at things in a different light; and it may be said that he did not hog all the credit for himself. He remembered George Cramer to such good effect that the latter was reinstated at Scotland Yard in his old position.

With Markheim dead there was no object in proceeding against the mestizos who had been roped in at the stables. They were kept in custody and charged with being concerned in Markheim's crimes. But this was only to ensure their deportation which took place shortly after.

By the time Markheim's affairs were thoroughly investigated by Scotland Yard a pretty good idea of the whole vast scheme was linked up with the affair of years before in South America, and, in this, Romer Walmsley laid all his cards on the table.

Mrs. Markheim was allowed to remain at the house where the final scene in her long life of tragedy and misery had taken place, and, with her, was Julia de Santos. Carlotta was buried near at hand, as was Junius Markheim, and it was Walmsley who suggested that the macaw had better be laid beside his mistress. From the moment she had fallen to the floor he had clung to her, savagely tearing at anyone who approached, and Blake agreed that it was the only kind thing to do. He left it to Walmsley to carry out this duty, and the latter would have been less than human had he not felt a strange relief when he knew the sinister bird that had hated him so was out of mischief for ever.

Walmsley also put in most of his time at the house, watching over the two women although Blake had sent down a trained nurse to watch Julia while she struggled back from the fantastic world into which the dope that Carlotta had given her had kept her a prisoner.

But, from time to time, when Blake drove down to see how things were progressing he noticed an increasing air of proprietorship on Walmsley's part, and smiled inwardly, for he could see how things were going. But he said nothing until one evening in the garden, when

Julia was quite herself again, she took his arm and tried to thank him for what he had done.

He put it off with a smile and mentioned Walmsley, and knew then from her telltale blushes that his intuition had not betrayed him. Nor was he surprised when, some three months later, Walmsley came to him and asked him to attend with him on a certain date at the chapel of the Spanish church, in London. Blake had already placed the girl's affairs in the hands of a competent jewel broker in London, and he was glad enough that she would have Walmsley to lean on in the future, for he was satisfied that Walmsley's metamorphosis was complete.

And he was not altogether unprepared for the announcement that Mrs. Markheim was to accompany them to South America, and make her home with them. She had done much for Julia under difficult circumstances, and, despite her stony manner, had a deep affection for the girl. Slowly she seemed to be changing, to be absorbing outside impressions for the first time in many years, and Blake felt optimistic that with Markheim no longer on the scene to outrage her every feeling, she would yet get something out of life. He was right, as later events proved.

THE END.
[43500 WORDS]

A Prison Treadmill . . . /drf

Not Guilty

By a Popular Author.

Complete Prison Yarn.

Chapter 1.   A Game of Draughts.

IN the great wholesale drapery house of Drummond, Lisle & Company business was over for the day; the staff, salesmen, and juniors were upstairs on the top floors amusing themselves according to their inclinations.

George Hastings, one of the juniors, a chubby, merry-faced fellow, was one of the youths who stood at the window, looking out into the sloppy street, a long drop below, and wishing that the great sulky cloud overhanging the rain was something that could be punched in the eye.

Then he turned from the window to watch the game of draughts that was progressing between Dick Burroughs and Gifford Ungley on the long table of the room. The game was now reduced to a battle of three kings on both sides, and George became interested —so much so that his sanguine, lively, and enthusiastic temperament became as keen and as full of flutter as though the contest was his own. As he watched he saw that Burroughs, who was a less skilled player than Ungley, was about to make a move that would deliver all his three kings to his opponent.

"Tchah! Not that, Dick! He'll swoop the lot!" he exploded eagerly, quite carried away, and feeling himself in a tremble. But he was wrong, and swiftly he realised it, and with an apologetic manner he exclaimed again quickly: "I am sorry, Ungley; I shouldn't have said it, I know, but I clean forgot myself."

"You always do clean forget yourself!" he snarled. "It's a way you have!" And in a sudden gust of passion he snatched up a draughtsman and flung it at George's face.

George and Ungley eyed each other steadily.

"For less than a cough-drop I'd pull your nose," he sneered viciously.

"Tut, tut, Ung'!" laughed several of the chaffers. "You can't pull a door-knob!" This shot seemed to exasperate Ungley into exhibiting his powers of annihilation, for he snatched up the draught-board, jumped to his feet, and flung the board and the draughtsmen on it at George's head.

George ducked down, and the missiles went flying at the wall behind him. But board and draughtsmen had hardly clattered to the floor before he had vaulted over the table, had planted his fist fairly and squarely on Ungley's nose, and had sent the ill-tempered churl flying with his head on the floor and his heels in the air.

"That ain't grass, Ungy; it's linoleum!"

The onlookers were enjoying themselves in high glee with Ungley's discomfiture, giving him back his own farmyard references in a new form, and baiting him unmercifully.

To have been knocked down before the crowd was enough, but to be badgered by the crowd in addition was maddening. Ungley scrambled to his feet in blind rage, dashed at George with a wild lunge, and— well, once more he went down, as the spectators merrily crowed "Kerwollop!" George's arm shot out, and stiffened like a ram as his fist again found Ungley's nose. Bash!

Now that he was stretched out a second time the sour biped was in no hurry to get up. Instead, his interest in his nose was pathetic. He dabbed it very tenderly; it was very soft, and very red —sloppily red.

George had won, but —well, every act has its consequence.

Chapter 2. Three Mouths Later.

THREE months passed. In all that time George and Ungley never once spoke to each other, except in the way of business, which involved compulsion, and left them with no choice.

But a greater evil than enmity was hovering over "the house." Once more business was finished for the day. It was a day in which George had again been in "hot water"; in fact, since his pummelling of Ungley there had hardly seemed to be two consecutive days when he was not in trouble, and when his superiors were not finding fault with him, and complaining of his errors and irregularities.

Although George's superiors did not know it, Ungley was very careless. He was always making mistakes, always doing wrong things, which had the appearance on the surface of having been committed by George, and George received the blame, the fault-finding, and the constant reports to the heads of the firm.

From being a sunny, willing, and smart fellow, George became miserable, dull, and slow. Sometimes he was even moody and morose, and his life became so irksome and unbearable that he even wrote a letter, intended for his home, in which he complained that his daily round had become so hateful that he would hardly be sorry if the whole place was burnt down and he was burnt in it.

But the letter had been written in a fit of gloom, and having "slept on it," as the old saying goes, he did not post it after all.

The fateful letter he had written in the evening, finishing it just before the regulation time for "lights out." All through the night the staff of the great business house again slept safely and well, but George opened his eyes with the morning, finding himself more than ever low in spirits and rebellious against his disagreeable lot.

Perhaps this was the reason that throughout the day's work things went more awkwardly and perversely with him than ever they had done before, until at last he threw down his pen recklessly. He had flung it to fall in the groove between the pages of the open day-book in which he was entering the day's sales; but the penholder fell askew, and instead of lodging in the groove, with its nib projecting from the top of the book, it rolled down one of the figured pages, trailing it with a river of ink from top to bottom.

"It's no use trying!" he exclaimed, irritable and weary. "I hate the place, and I don't care how soon I am out of it!"

From this outburst there could be only one effect. George was "carpeted" before the principal partner of the firm, and that evening all the "house" knew that he had received notice to leave.

But this was not the climax. There was worse to come. That night the great premises of Drummond, Lisle & Company were actually burned to the ground.

And George had discovered the fire! Troubled by the events of the miserable day, he had slept only fitfully, and his rousing shout it was that awakened the sleepers to the jeopardy.

By this time all the ground floors were ablaze, and the flames were leaping up so furiously that the sound sleepers and the slumberers, almost overpowered by the smoke, escaped to the adjoining roofs with the fire at their very heels. Fifteen fire-engines were now at work in the street below, but nothing could save the doomed building.

Of all the men and youths who escaped, George alone wore all his clothes, except his collar and tie. His garments were unbuttoned and his boots were unlaced, but all his raiment was on his back.

Then came inquiry. From the nature of the blaze the fire experts did not think that it had been accidental. The flames had begun their work in the basement. Had any employee of the house been down there after work had ended for the day?

Yes; George Hastings had been there. Every man and youth had to answer a searching battery of questions, and presently it leaked out that George was suspected of having fired the premises. Gifford Ungley had had to say that he had seen George coming from the basement as he went out to buy some cigarettes; but he did not say that he himself had gone below on his return, spitefully concerned to discover whether he could see for what purpose George had gone into the basement. He was a coward.

George could not deny that he had entered the department in which the fire was kindled. He had gone there, he said, to get something that he had forgotten, and had left in the pocket of his working jacket; but he did not like to say that that something was the letter he had written to his home.

The next minute he was being searched, and the fatal letter was found in his pocket.

Soon his worst fears were realised. He was given in charge of the police; from police-court he was committed for trial at the Old Bailey, and from the Old Bailey he went to a sentence of eighteen months' imprisonment with hard labour. He protested his innocence; but all the circumstances, all the evidence against him, especially his own letter, were convincing.

"You may consider yourself very fortunate that you are not standing here on a charge of manslaughter, or worse," said the judge, in sentencing him.

Soon he was put to work on "the mill." There was no pity for him. In this hell of felony, where the same offenders were constantly in and out on "short term" sentences for petty crimes, the warders were stricter and harsher than they were in a convict settlement. Continual acquaintance with the same prisoners brought them insensibly into a condition of mind in which they regarded the creatures around them as "a hopelessly bad lot," unworthy of anything but the hardest severity.

Poor George suffered the agonies of martyrdom. "The mill" looked quite easy when he started his spell upon it. There were broad arrows upon his knee breeches; but what did that matter? His legs felt much freer in knickerbockers than in trousers, and he would only have to step from one "paddle" to another as the wheel went round.

Pluckily he started, but soon he was in agony. The muscles if his legs tightened with the excruciating pain, and felt like cracking; the veins swelled and stood out on his forehead, and the sweat poured from him until his prison shirt was soaking wet.

For three-quarters of an hour George toiled, and then he could hardly keep his hold upon the bar. All his body felt as if it was breaking, and his agony of mind was as fearful as the racking strain of his limbs. No strength seemed to be left in him, and he had an awful mixture of sensations; he could feel the drag and weight of his own body, and yet it seemed to be sinking from it. His feet were like lead, and his arms were like flesh and muscles being torn with red-hot hooks. With each laboured tread, in each agonised moment, he felt that he would drop, and fall with his legs through the paddles of the hideous wheel.

"You pitiless brutes!" moaned George again.

"What's that?" challenged the warder. "A week's bread and water will be the price of that, with a double dose of 'mill' to follow. No impudence, now!" he added sharply, seeing that George's face was dropped back over his left shoulder, as if he turned his head in order to give fling to something he was about to say.

"It would take a patent double-buster to give you impudence." muttered a voice a box or two away. "You were right in front when sauce was given out, and nobody else got much."

"Who spoke there?" demanded the warder wrathfully under this outrage to his self-importance. "Stop the wheel!"

"I did —and hang you!" retorted the desperate fellow. "Do you think I care for a brute like you in this menagerie? I may as well be hanged for a sheep as for a lamb. Give me any of your bully, and I'll spread you out like a brace of ticks!"

By this time the treadmill-shed was in ugly commotion; the prisoners were ominously idle, edging from their boxes; and the warder was foaming angrily. George himself had fallen at last; and as he lay on the floor, with his head and shoulders in the gangway, he could see the bold violator of prison discipline.

"Tony!" he cried faintly. "Is it you, old chap?"

"Yes, it's me right enough, Hastings," returned Tony Trumble, an old schoolfellow whom George had recognised. "And pluck up, young 'un. If he comes any more nonsense with you, I'll bung his peepers!"

Chapter 3.   The Assault.

NATE GRIMSHAW, the warder, was a true prophet, for the good reason that he had a large hand in the successful engineering of his own prophecy. On his report and evidence before the governor, George and Tony saw no more of each other for a week. For this, also, there was a good, all-powerful reason. Both George and Tony were having an uninterrupted diet of bread and water, and they were in close confinement for seven days.

But even weeks have their endings, and presently George and Tony were back again at their prison labour. George had thought much of Tony during his seven days' of solitude; it had hurt him to find his old schoolfellow in the gaol, and it had hurt him still more to know that Tony, unlike himself, was a felon through crime actually committed. He had no proof that his conclusion was well founded, for he had had no opportunity of conversing with his old friend; but in Tony's recklessness he seemed to read everything that could be revealed.

Poor Tony! How had he come to fall so low? George was restless to discover the particulars of the story, and at last he found an opportunity to satisfy his craving. He was taking an hour's tramp in the stony, brick-walled exercise yard, and was moving in a circle of prisoners walking in Indian file, each man following three paces behind the fellow in front of him. It was punishment to speak; but it happened that George was walking in the wake of Tony, and, speaking low in his throat, he contrived to send his voice to Tony's ear.

"How was it, Tony?" he asked.

"Helped myself to a little. Meant to pay it back. Found I couldn't," was Tony's answer.

"What did you get?"

"Two years. Done six months. What's yours?"

"Eighteen months —for arson."

"Did you do it?"

"No."

"Well, then," replied George, "pull yourself together, and never say die."

Then there was silence, and suspicion in the glance of the warder's eye.

"Now then, there; keep your distance, No. 37!"

The prisoner of that number was slouching round in the ring irregularly in impudent bravado. He was a foul scoundrel, whom the warder, who was not a bad fellow, had reported justly for insolence and insubordination on a past occasion; and now, as No. 37's tramp brought him close to his custodian, he dashed out from the circle and struck him a murderous blow with something that he held in his hand.

Instantly the filing prisoners broke their formation and leapt willingly into disorder. George and Tony both saw the blow delivered, and now they realised that the warder was full length on the ground, that the burly ruffian was on top of him, and that he was in a fair way to be killed.

Swiftly as the desperado had leapt upon the warder, George and Tony now sprang upon him. A wound was in the victim's forehead, and blood was streaming from it, while the felonious wild beast hammered fresh blows at his face with the weapon that he held in his hand.

But now the tugging hands of George and Tony were on him, tearing, clinging, and dragging at his head and shoulders and his windmill arms. While Tony flung his arms round the brute's neck and dragged him back, George seized his clenched fist and wrenched away the weapon that it gripped. The thing was an ugly instrument for mischief —a scrap of rusty hoop-iron which the ruffian had somehow managed to find and secrete.

Having secured the weapon, George delivered a smashing, undercutting blow in the wretch's face as Tony dragged it back from the prostrate warder, not with the cowardly iron, but with his own honest fist. The lowest of the prisoners who saw the blow instantly leapt into brutish rage, and charged at the courageous fellows, to kick and batter them into insensibility.

But George was as quick-witted as he was swift; he pounced at the warder's weapon, seized it, and flourished it around, keeping the beasts at bay, while Tony struggled with the savage who had created the mutiny.

"Warders! Warders!" he shouted, sending his voice in a pitch to carry far and wide.

And then, seeing that the murderous No. 37 had fought to his feet, and was about to kick Tony below the belt, he leapt aside and brought his weapon swinging down on the scoundrel's charging foot. Instantly the wretch toppled to the ground with a wild yell, clutching at the wound across his foreleg. The limb was cut to the bone.

"Keep back!" cried George, flashing his weapon in all directions.

But he had no need to prolong his shouting; the warders of the prison came running to the charge, and in a few minutes the violent outbreak was quelled.

Thanks to George, Tony had accomplished the first act in his redemption. The governor of the prison commended him and George warmly, promising to report their conduct to the Home Secretary, in the hope that he would remit them three months each from their sentences.

Chapter 4. George's Release.

"Och, y're a baste! Bad luck to yez! Oi'd loike to spell murther in Oirish to yez, I wud, ye son uv a spalpeen!"

The speaker was Rory O'Shanaghan, and he was here in the local prison on account of the rather mixed notions he had on the subject of what belonged to him and what belonged to other people, he had been doorkeeper of the "house" door at the premises of Drummond, Lisle & Company; but because of his lamentable inability to distinguish the firm's property from his own —though that property had taken the form of rolls of cloth, which he had purloined and sold to a "trader" —he was here to improve this understanding by the process of doing six months' "hard."

But another employee of Drummond, Lisle & Co. had preceded him, and that employee was Gifford Ungley. The author of George's downfall, it seemed, had been promoted to a desk in the cashier's department, and he had taken advantage of his advancement to defraud the firm of considerable sums of money. So glaringly graceless had been his embezzlements that he had been sentenced to two years' hard labour.

In his adjoining cell George laughed, in spite of himself, as he heard the Irishman's voice. Nothing could suppress the loquacious Rory when once his tongue took possession of him, and insisted on wagging; not all the prison governors and warders in Christendom could stop him. And George laughed the more because he knew what was happening. The door of his own cell had just been opened by a warder, who, attended by the prisoner doing fatigue duty, had delivered to him his breakfast of bread and skilly. Who should the fatigue duty prisoner be but Gifford Ungley! The warder and his attendant were now in Rory's cell, and George could see the scene as well as if no walls were between him and the Irishman's unappreciated company.

"I shall report you for this!" intimated the warder, in a chippy tone.

"Begorra!" pranced Rory afresh. "Ray-port, is ut? Rayport yir gran'mither, sorr, an' bad cess to yez both! Oi wudn't lit my pig be seen in the saime county wid yez — ut's too illigint to look at yez across a ten mile bog, bedad! Soilence! Rayport! Go an' boil ut, an' ate ut!"

"You had better get out," directed the warder to the attendant Ungley. "Your face evidently doesn't agree with him."

"Saint Patrick, he'd betther, or he'll only nade a hearse an' a tombshtone!" Rory recommended. "An' they would be too much loike Wistminsther Abbey for him! Wasn't Oi afther say in ut was through him that George Hashtings was putt away, bedad? Didn't he cause the foire himself, the green-eyed frog uv a bog? Whoy did Oi have futs? Didn't he go down afther Hashtings, the spalpeen, an' lave the gas burrnin' undher the cloths left hangin' on the rods, baycourse no mither's son sushpected that the gas wud be lit any more?"

"Are you talking about me?" George heard Ungley dare to ask.

"Oi belave Oi was," Rory returned, in a queer way, as if he thought it was possible he might have been talking in his sleep. "Bejabers, I belave I was callin' yez the larrst snake in Oireland that was sint over to this divvil av a counthry. An' if ut's not loikin' ut ye are, arrah! ye can have this!"

George heard a splash, followed by a splutter and a smash, and he knew what had happened. Rory had shied the hot gruel in his basin slap into Ungley's face, and the embezzler, in his sudden astonishment, had dropped all the breakfasts he was carrying.

At once there was a hubbub in the prison-ward, and George himself added to it by knocking at his cell-door.

"You heard it, sir —you heard it!" he exclaimed excitedly to the warder when his door was opened. "Thank Heaven, at last my innocence is proved! Take me to the governor, sir."

"Against regulations, Hastings," replied the warder. "You must wait till he comes round on inspection at ten."

"But I shall be at work then," suggested George urgently.

"No, you won't," was the answer. "The governor will be told, and you will be brought back to your cell. If that daft Irishman's story is right, so much the better for you."

It was right, and two days later, on the forced confession made by Ungley that George was guiltless of having caused the Drummond-Lisle fire, an order was received from the Home Office directing George Hastings to be released. Better still, the world was not harsh to George when he returned to it; his old firm invited him back with sincere regret for the wrong and injustice that had been done him, and reinstated him gladly in the old office.

The End.

Our Magazine Corner.

Crooks' Inventions.

NECESSITY was ever the mother of invention, and with the criminal fraternity this applies perhaps more than anywhere else. Fresh forces and situations make it necessary for the crook to use all his ingenuity to cope with the rapid progress of his enemies, both inside and outside the law. Often he is more afraid of his own kidney than the police.

Possibly the most harassed crooks in the world are the bootlegger and the smuggler. As soon as one bright scheme is working successfully for outwitting the police or hijackers who are hot on the trail, someone gets wind of it, an antidote is found, and the crooks must turn their brains in other directions.

One bright idea of an American bootlegging gang was the use of torpedoes filled with illicit liquor. These were shot off landwards to be picked up by their confederates and the contents dealt with in the usual way. This was successful for a long time until a revenue cutter got in the way and then the gang had to think of something else.

American gangsters lead a hectic existence at the best of times, and their brainpower is always working overtime on new devices for their own protection.

They have always paid a considerable attention to their motor-cars. Al Capone, for instance has a car, the body of which is made entirely of armour plate, and fitted with bullet-proof glass windows. The whole weighs eight tons, generally resembles a miniature tank and has saved Al's life on numerous occasions. It cost thirty thousand dollars.

A motor-car belonging to New York gangsters was captured recently by the police and found to be fitted with a complete device for ejecting poison gas from the exhaust. A tank was fitted beneath the chassis with a tube leading into the exhaust pipe, and by means of a lever on the dash-board, the driver could operate his terrible weapon with ease while travelling at speed.

Before the car was captured, the gangster allowed the policeman who was chasing him on a motor-cycle to get quite close to him, then opened the valve and shot a cloud of poison gas into the cop's face. The policeman lost control of his motor-cycle and crashed into a ditch.

Only a short while ago another car full of gangsters made its escape from the police in a thick smoke-cloud ejected from the rear of the car. By the time it had cleared, the crooks had completely vanished.

Steel bullet-proof shirts have been worn by both gangsters and police for some time, but perhaps the prize for self-protection goes to a certain French criminal. Not only did he wear a bullet-proof shirt, but he wore special spiked armlets and shoulder straps, so that to tackle him in a hand to hand fight was rather like attacking a porcupine. He carried a knife, an automatic, and in each pocket a mills bomb. Quite a pleasant customer!

An example of the more subtle line along which a crook's ingenuity works was shown when Alberto Pinto, a notorious international bandit, was arrested some time ago on the Continent.

In his possession was found a document written in a strange language. For a long time he would say nothing about it, but at last he admitted that the language was one devised by an international gang of crooks in a mass conference at Lorida, Spain, in order that criminals present might communicate with each other without fear of detection. It is interesting to note that the Lorida conference was an attempt to amalgamate various national crook gangs into one huge concern —like one vast international trading company. Had it been successful, its ramifications would have been colossal.
S.S.

Interestingly, I searched for Alberto Pinto and could find nothing on the web! Similar results on the Lorida, Spain criminal conference! /drf

www.ingramcontent.com/pod-product-compliance
Lightning Source LLC
Chambersburg PA
CBHW031837170626
46807CB00004B/1502